Season of the Cicada

Susan Ellison

FOR MY CHILDREN

IN BUDDHISM, THERE ARE FOUR NOBLE TRUTHS. THEY ARE THE TRUTH OF SUFFERING, THE TRUTH OF THE CAUSE OF SUFFERING, THE TRUTH OF THE END OF SUFFERING, AND THE TRUTH OF THE PATH THAT LEADS TO THE END OF SUFFERING. THE EIGHT FOLD PATH IS THE PATH THAT LEADS TO THE END OF SUFFERING. THE WHEELED-FIGURE BELOW OUTLINES THE EIGHT FOLD PATH.

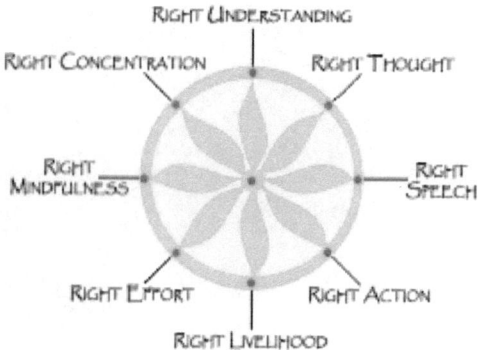

PROLOGUE

"I don't think I love you anymore." The words spin over and over in her head like a vinyl record skipping on the groove mistakenly cut diagonally between seemingly concentric circles. "We've changed... better off apart..." She removes the satchel that carries her passport, walks towards the forest with the knowledge that no eyes follow her. She will walk far enough to be lost, separated from the group. By the time she regrets the choice, she will be too far from the camp to find her way back.

After an hour, she comes upon a cliff. Walking up to the edge, she kicks some rocks by accident and hears the echoing hollow sound as they fall below. She remembers skydiving and needing the instructor to jump tandem with her. She never would have the courage to jump by herself. Now she is certain of the courage to end her own life deliberately; courage fueled by the betrayal of the man she loves. His disregard is the push of the instructor, and she will gladly fall away.

She has hit rock-bottom, the fall is incidental. She knows that she can never return to the mere fantasy of her demise again. She walks to the edge of the cliff, where the strong wind rips at her, drying her tears. One unbalancing move, and she will fall to the violent foam covered rocks below, and wash out to sea. She will never have the courage again to stare a deliberate death in the face. If she walks away now, she will not have the courage again to stand in this place. Her lips and tongue are too dry to taste the salt from her tears. Like other times before, she calls for the wisdom of her deceased grandmother. At other times, she swore she could hear her voice. Yet today, only silence, her desperation so great she cannot imagine what she or anyone could possibly say to save her.

THE JOURNEY

CHAPTER ONE

SUSQUEHANNA RIVER VALLEY, PENNSYLVANIA
MARCH, 2012

I'm not sure how I got to this place, a farm in central Pennsylvania, planting a spring garden; the cancer of fear in my body multiplying with great fervor. My son and my husband are waiting at bay in a city that swallows them whole. I escaped the metal-framed, concrete landscape for this one. The rolling Pocono Mountains flow away from me. Frosty dawns melt to gray mornings. I am with my friend. She is the one who makes the knowledge of suffering her safe haven. I can be with her, who does not deny my reality. She accepts the place in which I stand today. Perhaps through osmosis, in standing beside her, I will also come to a place of acceptance.

These are the things I am grateful for: the life of my son, lightly fried zucchini blossoms *that* summer in Tuscany, juicy strawberries from the farmer's market on Thursday afternoons, and the memory of spring showers of cherry blossoms that seemed to fall endlessly from ancient trees lining the Shinano River in Tokyo.

In life, we carry with us the memories of the dreams that never did come true. I pray in silence that these memories will not stay with me when I leave this world. They are the hell within which I have entrapped myself for too long. Regret, unrequited loves, and cowardice choices.

I longed for adventure, once. And in my longing, I found loneliness and more longing. Discontent characterized my days of adventure. I sought true love, honesty, and idealism. When my life became filled with a husband, his family and our son, I longed for the voice of freedom my own choices had silenced long ago. Romantic afternoons of parallel worlds filled my unease, and I was left to wonder in the midst of the responsibilities and obligations I was defined by. Slowly, over years of deliberate choices, my voice was silenced and I lost any sense of who I was.

Perhaps the loneliness that I feel is simply the culmination of my rotting dreams. And yet, it might be the spark that leads me to search for life again. This I will only realize sometime from now, as I work in a temple garden just outside of Tokyo, in the afternoon's last light. Sixteen years ago I stood before family and friends and committed a lifetime to another, and now I find that I am unable to fulfill that pledge. My desires have been silenced by his. The despair that I am now living is actually the force that will show me how I have wronged my own life, believing for so many years that I could have lived differently. It will lead me back to the paths I have taken, and like slow motion frames flashing before my eyes, I will be given the chance to live life again.

Dai-en waits for me by a white mini-van at the train station. She is dressed in the traditional white robe characteristic of a Zen Buddhist monk. More than the shrouds that cover her body, the newly shaven head

8

draws attention to her in the rural Pennsylvania setting. We could be anywhere – in western Japan at a station along a local line. We touch hands in embrace and Dai-en helps me to lift my suitcase into the van. The chill in the air is real but the morning sun has already melted the frost to a shiny coverlet. The fields stand ready to awaken to shades of green. It is late March and spring is just beginning to find its way to this place.

The short drive to Dai-en's farm takes less than ten minutes. On the way, Dai-en tells me about the developer who has purchased Mt. Lido. He has plans to build more than two hundred new vacation condominiums at the base of the mountain. The western side of the development will butt up against her property line, and disturb the colony of snow owls who reside in the trees.

"One of the females gave birth to at least five babies last month."

"Really? How did you discover them?"

"I saw them yesterday evening when I walked out to mark the fields for spring planting. They were already learning to fly. The sun had barely set and they were hopping along the frozen grass."

"What will happen to them if this development starts?"

"I don't know. I wish I could tell you that they would just move to the other end of the farm, but that's unlikely. They will probably just leave this area altogether."

"Yeah, I guess if they sense danger, they would be inclined to just take off, find a new place."

"I understand the need for money but the owls don't. Their needs are much simpler – the trees where they live, the mice in the fields, and the sky above."

"Like children. Remember that innocence?" I hear my own voice trail off and I go into my thoughts.

"Mmm. How about you?"

"No, I can't remember anything simple now. I search William's eyes but even he has grown years beyond simplicity. We have tainted him in so many ways."

It is a short drive to the farm. The front gate is broken at the hinges, probably the result of heavy snowfall. Smoke billows from the chimney towards the skeletal oak that rises above the main house. A feeling of coming home surprises me. It has been years since I was last here.

Warm tea greets us in the simple *tatami* room off the kitchen in Dai-en's house.

"So, let's get to the big questions. How are you my friend?"

"I am okay. Sometimes one day at a time is too long, you know?"

"Have you tried one breathe at a time?"

I smile to know the wisdom of my friend. The whole concept of being aware of each of my breaths seems so foreign to me now, as most of the time I feel like I'm hyperventilating. My skepticism envies the simplicity of her world: no husband, no in-laws, no children to disappoint, no hurt, and no regret. In admiring Dai-en's solitary life, I ignore her suffering. I know that everyone suffers, it is just difficult for me to see anybody but myself these days.

"I guess that's why I'm here. I need to be reminded of my breath." Tears well-up in my eyes. I feel so much pain now. Guilt overwhelms me most days. How could I have failed like this?

CHAPTER TWO

SUSQUEHANNA RIVER VALLEY, PENNSYLVANIA
MARCH, 2012

"Come. Let's put your things in your room and go to visit the garden."

The wooden stairs creak under my feet, as we ascend to the second floor. I am encased in warm hues of timber; the walls are a slightly darker version of the same wood under my feet. The steep staircase turns sharply to the left. My bag weighs heavily on my arm. Dai-en carries herself deliberately and with much ease, even in the heavy cotton monk's kimono she dons. Warm sunlight filters into the room we enter. The vibrant red duvet is a splash of color, in contrast to the warm wooden walls. Simple, gauze curtains billow in the wind that blows gently through the window. The air is chilled and crisp. Dai-en mumbles an apology, glides across the floor, and closes the wooden framed panes of glass.

"Take your time, Elise. I will be shucking beans at the kitchen sink. Come join me and we'll walk the garden together."

"Thank you, Dai-en… for everything."

She smiles warmly at me and pauses. "It is good you came."

The overstuffed leather chair in the window seems indulgent but I cannot resist. The worn hide envelopes me and I immediately feel the heat from the sun on my cheeks.

She is asleep by the fireplace in their Manhattan apartment. She is awoken by laughter that she doesn't recognize. Peeking her head around the heavy chair arms, Alan's eyes lock hers in surprise and horror. She hears a shuffling of feet in the hallway. The front door opens and closes. A long pause follows the closing door, Alan enters the room and sits across from her. Salt is streaming down her face in disbelief. His defeated eyes shift from hers to the floor in front of him. There is nothing to say and yet so much to know and feel and deny. He didn't expect her to return from their house in the Hamptons until Friday afternoon.

I must have fallen to sleep for a few minutes. The sun has tucked behind the mountain. I leave my bag and head back down the narrow wooden staircase. Dai-en is just finishing the beans, wipes her damp hands on the kitchen towel, and turns towards me.

"Let's head out to the garden. Did you find everything you need?"

"It's just perfect." I try to forget my liminal dream, the product of a not-too-distant memory. When I was a teenager, my mother accused me of wearing rose colored glasses, of not seeing people for who they really are. While I know that I don't need to sketch a picture of my life for Dai-en, exhaustion fuels my inability to reveal tonight all that it contains.

We pass through the backdoor to a field that sprawls into the distance, until it touches the base of the mountains. A single, large oak spans the backyard. A row of three picnic tables sits beneath its summer shade for retreat meals.

12

"This way, Elise."

I follow Dai-en to the south side of the house where a freshly tilled garden stands. The perfectly mounded rows sit waiting for the miraculous seeds of spring to be sown. The compost festers into the mineral clad soil, dark, rich, ripe. Dai-en walks slowly and deliberately to the edge of the dark sea and points towards a make-shift greenhouse in the distance. Heavy, semi-translucent, plastic tarps are drawn tightly across a sturdy bamboo frame.

"My nephew comes every spring break to rebuild the structure and help me plant my seedlings."

"Where does your family live?" I ask hesitantly, knowing I have been told before.

"Cleveland. Cold city."

"Yes. Will you show me the sprouts?" An excitement flutters in my stomach, like butterflies. When William was young, I planted a vegetable garden with him each year. I was motivated by the excitement on his face when he first spotted a sprout pushing its tiny leaves through the surface of the soil. When he discovered the first yellow summer squash flower under the oversized green leaves, he would shriek with delight. The pride on William's face when he carried the first ripe tomato to the kitchen for dissection fueled my love of the garden.

"A seed will wither and die if left in the sun."

I look into my friend's eyes and a faint smile appears on my face, in anticipation of the lesson I am about to receive.

"The seed's fate is the same whether it withers to nothing in the sun or it sprouts and blossoms into a zucchini, only to die and be sown as compost into the end of season soil." Dai-en pauses for a moment and raises her gaze to meet my eyes.

"Does it matter which path the seed's fate follows?"

"You tell me. Does the journey matter? Long, short, wealth, growth, purpose. If we're just going to die in the end, does it really matter what happens in between?"

"Yes, of course."

"Why?"

I pause to think about her question. "Because everyone wants to live a good life."

"Yes?" She pauses for a moment and then continues. "No matter what the life is like? Even if one is suffering emotionally or physically?"

"But we have choices. We can take care of ourselves, create a better life."

"Really?" She says with a knowing smile. I smile back.

"But some do not have choices - those dying of cancer for example."

"Just because their life is shortened, doesn't mean they don't have choices. There is a number of days for each of us, and none of us knows exactly how many. Whether we have 60 more days or 16,000, we have choices. What if each of us chose acceptance during that tenure?" Dai-en pauses and then asks me, "Do *you* have a choice?"

I pause knowing that the answer is obvious. "Yes, but sometimes I don't feel like I do."

"It's an illusion you know."

"What's that?"

"We think that one path is the right choice and one is wrong. It paralyzes us."

"That describes me perfectly: paralyzed."

"What we fail to realize is that both paths lead to the same result."

"You mean that we will die either way?"

"Essentially."

"Sounds morbid."

"Only because of our limited view. On some level we believe death is a choice, like we have a say in the matter. Our fear and our caution indicate that we think it's something we can negotiate. It's just a reality. The thing we can negotiate is our choice over *how* to live. Each moment, each day, the who, what, where, how – that's where our choices, our "say" in the matter, reside. The certainty of death doesn't have to be morbid. There is great possibility in its certainty."

"How so?"

"If life will end, that means our suffering is also temporary. And it also means our happiness is precious and must be enjoyed in the moment."

"This too shall pass?"

"Yes, something like that."

"You know, if you eat a zucchini blossom, it will never become a fruit. But, would you want to sacrifice the delicate, unique taste so that you could eat only fully mature zucchini all of the time?"

"Never. You can't compare the two. They are two totally different tastes."

"Exactly."

"But what about the seed?"

"Well, at least in this life, you and I have both made it past the seed withering in the sun phase."

"Although I have days when I'm sure that's what I am… a dried up seed."

"Elise, someday we will all be compost, pushing up daisies in the garden. Right? Rich, poor, beautiful, athletic. We all have the same fate. That's one thing that's for sure."

The twilight has turned to darkness. The first stars are appearing in the moonless sky.

"Okay, so we all end up dead, but what about life? If all life is suffering, then what's the point? I mean, how do we detach from the things and people we care so deeply about?"

"Maybe you should explore the things you care so deeply for. Seek to understand the nature of your relationships. What do you derive from your connections with people? Remember, that ultimately we are selfish beings. Our attachments are also selfish. Can you think of a relationship that isn't about you?"

"William."

"Are you sure?" Dai-en pauses, looking into my eyes, as I think about my son. "Do you remember why you and Alan chose to have him in your lives?"

"We wanted to create a family, manifest our love, nurture and love another. We felt we had something to give."

"All of these things are beautiful, but they are also in some way about you. What do you derive from your relationship with William?"

I think deeply about this: his love, the joy of sharing in the beginning of his life, his innocence, doing things differently than my parents did. I can't answer. Each of my thoughts inevitably traces back to me, my needs, and my insecurities. How could creating life and nurturing a child be an act of selfishness?

"Listen, Elise, the love and compassion you show William each day are not acts of selfishness, but

16

life is a series of teachings and the people we choose to have in our lives are like a roadmap to this learning."

"Why did you marry Alan?"

"Because I loved him. He was strong and confident about me. I wanted to support him and share life with him."

"Was that choice about him or about you?"

"I guess, ultimately about me. Being with him made me feel good about myself. Well, at least for a time." Thoughts flood my head. It is as though I chose Alan to fit the dialogue I had about myself ... not good enough, incomplete, something missing.

"Elise, keep in mind that, in order to create something, you must first have nothingness, otherwise we are simply living an extension of our past. When you arrive at emptiness, there is the possibility of creation. You have to lose your story, your interpretation of what life has meant in the past, to truly be present. When we are present, we are open to the possibilities the future holds. There isn't room for creation in a vessel that is already full."

"I never truly feel satisfied with my relationships. There is always something missing."

"What is the same about every relationship you have had?"

I pause to consider this question. Finally I answer, "Me?"

"That's right. So let's consider you. Are you up for it?"

"I just don't understand how this could be my fault? Alan is the one who destroyed our family."

"I didn't say that anything is your fault." Her eyes fill with tears of love and I feel utterly confused.

"I just think it might be worth exploring the question of you, instead of anybody else. Don't you think it's about time to make this about you?"

"Yes!" I blurt out spontaneously. "Finally, something in my life that's about me."

"Oh, don't mistake what I am saying. It has always already been about you. I just think we should look into the stories you are living so you can finally move into the present. If you choose to do this, I promise you great freedom from suffering.

"Detachment?"

"Exactly."

"I'm afraid to live 'detached.'"

"I know, but when you detach from the outcome, from your expectations about how it all should be, what flows in is love, deep profound love, for yourself and others. Imagine if you didn't have to control everybody and everything in your life. Imagine if you lived without having responsibility for everyone else's actions and choices. If that went away, what kind of a life would you live? Who would you become? Who would you choose to love?"

Blackness surrounds us now, a symphony of stars above, a chill in the air around us. I exhale deeply and watch crystals form in mid-air.

I follow Dai-en inside. We wash in the heavy metal sink in the mud-room. She washes her hands and arms to the elbows, her face, the back of her neck, and rinses the inside of her mouth. I realize we are about to sit *zazen* before the evening meal.

Anticipating this weekend, I have been practicing sitting for the last few weeks. My head spins, my legs numb easily, and I am truly out of practice. Yet, I look forward to the moments of quiet like a glass of cold water after a day at the beach. In all of my loneliness over the last months, my life lacks quietude. The thoughts, regrets, and fears that fill my head have convinced me of who I am. My existence has come to be defined by these emotions; my sleepless nights and salty tears assure me that I am still alive. I have come to embody fear and regret; they have darkened the half circles under my eyes and carved crevices across my forehead. I wear the seeming meaninglessness of my life like fresh tattoos for all of the world to see.

My despair is only highlighted as acquaintances at the farmer's market or the grocery store comment on how great I look. "Have you lost weight? Who is your trainer? Where do you work out?" One day I even told the clerk at the checkout lane that she too could have my body. All she had to do was marry a man who would one day choose to leave. There was a time, not long ago, when I was compassionate, playful, and happy. Now I am a cynic, defined by anger and deep sadness.

The *tatami* feels smooth and cool under my bare toes. The lights are dim and the incense is strong. As I exhale deeply, Dai-en hits the side of a Tibetan singing bowl with a metal mallet. The sound resonates long and I think for a moment of the smallness of my life. Breathe in. Breathe out. I believe that if I sit long enough, if I fill my lungs with fresh air enough times, something will happen. So, I sit, and empty my mind of thoughts the best I can, and wait.

A rustle to the left of me concludes my meditation. Dai-en has stood gracefully and returned her *zabuton* to its pile. I sit for a long minute feeling the flow of blood return to my tingling legs. The feeling is almost unbearable and I cannot speak. Five minutes pass before I am able to stand. After placing my *zabuton* to the side of the doorway, I step into the hallway and head for the kitchen.

I help myself to rice and soup and sit across from my friend. She has already laid pickles and several dishes of green vegetables on the table between us. I smile to see a dish of cold tofu with grated ginger and green onion. Dai-en pours a tiny amount of soy sauce over the top. Our meal begins.

Our silent meal is a blessing. The awkwardness of quiet between two dining together is completely absent. In its place I feel the texture of my food – the creaminess of the tofu in contrast to the crunch of the mountain green vegetables. There is sweetness in its light sauce. I taste the sticky gluten on each kernel of rice, giving it firmness. We eat the green beans Dai-en shucked earlier, now pickled in rice vinegar. We sip the last tea from our cups, and clear the dishes.

While I unpack my simple things, Dai-en sits *zazen* once again in her room. I know she will wait until I have finished my bath before she will take hers. I descend the stairs again, walk down the hall and push the *noren* curtain aside to enter the bath room. Lifting the wooden cover of the bath, steam flows into my nose. I shower quickly, anticipating the hot soaking water. Fragrant rosemary floating on top of the water fills the air. After 20 minutes I take my reddened body upstairs and fall into a dreamless slumber.

CHAPTER THREE

SUSQUEHANNA RIVER VALLEY, PENNSYLVANIA
MARCH, 2012

The time I sit *zazen* is excruciating, no longer because of my limp legs, but because it is the time I turn inward to face the demons in my head. Fear consumes my every thought. There is no room in my banter for love, peace, or insight. I long to be folding sheets, weeding the garden or picking through grains of rice. But time with Dai-en is not like this. She is present and exudes a sense of calm, but this practice creates a space for the demons in my head to surround me and cackle at this life I walk through like a lonely ghost, caught between worlds. The energy in the room flows towards her, and with loving compassion she seems to reach back to touch me. I long to be more like her, and in my longing I elude that which she embodies.

Bucknell University
October, 1990

The floor in the inner sanctuary of the university church is cold. A small water feature spits liquid to the rocks below. Her thoughts trickle to nothingness. Her breath becomes avoidable. Her heartbeat slows. The clock clicks once and, another minute later, again before fresh air fills her lungs.

Later when the silence is broken by Dai-en's gentle voice she realizes her accomplishment. She takes this knowledge to the university green where later that evening she lay quietly next to Max. They are star gazing again. This confidence spills over into her life; tonight she does not lie questioning his thoughts. Instead she peers through the holes in the sky, enamored with the perfection of the universe. It is one of those fleeting moments when she believes everything in her life will be alright no matter what happens next. It is always at these moments when he is suddenly attracted to her. Max reaches over and touches her hand. She responds with a finger entwining embrace and smiles. She will learn only years later that she reads into everything too much. He simply is; and sometimes his thoughts are silent. She was never able to appreciate his inner quietness. She was always too busy listening to the voice of her own insecurities.

The grass is becoming wet under their bodies and they decide to head home. Home is a small, lofted room in a quieter corner of his fraternity. The ritual begins. Max lights a stick of cherry infused incense. Cocteau Twins spins out of the disc player. They talk, imagining the hills of Oregon, and remembering the day they climbed along a ridge overlooking the Columbia River. Wind surfers skated across the glass water below. Cool gusts chilled the sweat on their brows.

For now, his love is simple, uncluttered and honest. Guiding her towards his overstuffed chair in the corner beyond the microwave, he sits. She finds his legs beneath her and she smiles at perfection of the moment.

"It smells good. Is it from Japan?"

"Yeah. I brought it back."

"I like it. What is the scent?" she asks as she reaches for the box on top of the microwave.

"Sa-ku-ra. What does that mean?"

"Cherry blossom."

"Hmm."

22

Her favorite part of the day is when she is lost in his slumber. The music is loud but she drifts easily to sleep in his arms.

CHAPTER FOUR

SUSQUEHANNA RIVER VALLEY, PENNSYLVANIA
MARCH, 2012

I sit by myself at the kitchen table sipping tea, longing to belong to this place. The dishes have each found their way back to their home on the shelf, and I am staring out at the grey sky which borders the horizon at the far edge of the field. Loneliness overwhelms me.

Dai-en comes in from the garden. I look up at her, blinking tears from my eyes.

"Oh, Elise. My dear friend."

"I had a memory come up during our meditation this morning."

"Tell me."

"It was around the time we first met. Bucknell. Max. Just that I should have chosen him. I was so insecure then. I just wanted to be wanted."

"Elise, we don't make wrong choices. Good, bad, right, wrong. We make choices. That's all. And we continue on the journey, creating meaning. We need to be aware of the meaning we are creating. Were you ready to be married to Max at age 22?"

"Oh my gosh, no. It would have been a disaster."

"Again, right, wrong. You would have learned what you needed to learn or another situation would have presented itself to inform your journey."

"So, you're saying we don't have a choice?"

"Of course you do, Elise. You have many. It is just that life is not so linear, so black and white. You have to allow for the gray, the part that isn't all figured out and perfect."

My head is filled with confusion and I feel like I cannot think anymore.

"The lotus flower blossoms from sludge at the bottom of a gray and muddy pond. Beauty comes from the murkiness, the dark, silty places of life." Dai-en pauses for a moment to reach across the table to take my hand and force eye contact, wanting to be sure I really hear what she is saying. "No mud. No lotus."

With my hand still in hers, she breaks the silence, "So, will you stay to help me plant the garden in the morning?"

A simple "yes" to my friend, and I feel some purpose in my life, if only temporarily. How did Dai-en know what I was feeling? How could she provide such a simple solution?

"I have nowhere to go." I am sitting in the *zendo* with my legs hanging over the meditation platform. Dai-en is at my side. I have broken into tears at the end of our meditation.

"I remember a Leo Tolstoy children's story I read years ago. The edict was something like this: the best place for you to be is right where you are; the best thing for you to be doing is exactly what you are doing right now; and the best person for you to be with is the one beside you."

"Where do you long to be?"

I hesitate for a moment and then answer. "Japan." I know the answer before she asks. If someone had asked me the same question at any moment in the past twenty years, I would have given the exact answer, with the same hesitation, in exactly the same way.

"Ahh, yes." Dai-en smiles and nods in a knowing way.

"The lover. The love affair. She holds you gently, isolates you, makes you an island in your own soul. She holds you in a place where no one else can touch."

We smile to each other.

With that, Dai-en rises and disappears into the hallway.

I return to the kitchen to start the rice for our dinner. Staring at the phone on the wall, I know that I need to call Alan. William returns to New York tonight from a long weekend in Maine fishing with a friend's family. Since he was born, I have spoken with him every night we haven't been together. It has been difficult not to hear his voice for these three days. I tell myself I will call after I make the rice.

Every time I rinse the rice, I remember Mr. Tanemura teaching me how to prepare a meal the first evening I arrived in rural Japan to teach English for a year. He added just enough water to cover the kernels before showing me how to squeeze the rice in my fist. This process activated the glutens and ensured sticky, firm rice. Dump. Rinse again. I repeat the process 3 times, until the water runs nearly clear. I look at the phone again. I will call after the spinach is finished blanching. The citrus *yuzu* tree in the kitchen window is just beginning to bear fruit. I reach around to the sphere hanging closest to the sunny window. After cutting the fruit open and emptying the contents into a bowl, I add soy sauce, rice vinegar and a touch of sugar.

I squeeze the spinach to remove excess water and pile the clumps onto a small serving dish. The tangy *yuzu* sauce makes my mouth water as I smell the sweetened citrus essence pour over the leaves. A sprinkle of sesame seeds and I am left to look at the phone again.

"Elise!"

"Hi, Alan. Did Will make it home alright?"

"Yes, he got in about twenty minutes ago. And I'm fine too."

"Did he have a good time?"

"Yeah, I think so. Didn't say much. Caught a big one. Think he said it was a bass."

"Wow!"

"Elise, how are you?"

"I'm fine. Is he there now?"

"Ahh, yeah, well, I'll have to go get him. Let's see. I was just sitting down to the watch the game."

She is silent.

"Tell me about your weekend while I walk through."

"It's good. Good to see Dai-en."

"I hope she is giving you good advice."

"She is amazing. But it isn't really advice. She listens and helps me to see things."

"Does she know about us?"

"Yes."

"What does she say?"

"She just listens a lot. You know, Alan, I don't really want to talk about this right now. Alan, can you put William on the phone?"

"He's in the shower."

"Can you ask him to call me?"

"Of course."

"I need to go, Alan." I hang up the phone. I can feel the deep creases across my forehead, etched by sleepless nights and countless hours of outpouring in my therapist's office.

The rice is done. I sit at the kitchen table staring at the "keep warm" light, waiting for Dai-en. I try to convince myself that my eyes are wet from staring at the light. Foolish girl. I love to pretend everything is still perfect, that my world hasn't fallen apart. I try to remember simplicity and William running on the beach and Alan loving me with pride for giving life to our son. My mind stretches far to recall our first kiss, the adoration I felt flow from his eyes to mine. However lost in the memories of us I can find myself, the sudden rush of his words of wanting to end our marriage makes me feel lost and utterly alone.

In my dreams he is laughing at me. I am a fool. I wake in a puddle of sweat, squinting in the dark to focus on anything other than the images in my dream. The blackness stares back at me and mocks my singularity. Death has found me and I take solace in the nothingness. Finally, the pain will go away. The butterflies in my stomach assure me, the peace of death has not yet arrived. This world will be my hell, and if I am going to choose not to participate in this life, it will take more effort than merely waking to nothingness in the middle of the night. I indulge my sorrow for a minute, embracing the thought that the world would be better off without me. Save William, that's the world I would choose to live in; a world without the pain that characterizes my life. While I recognize the only place without pain is death, I am not even sure how to get there. If I knew for sure that William would forgive my departure and someday meet me on the other side, I might choose to go.

Dai-en places a cup of tea in front of me. The steam jolts me back to this farm in central Pennsylvania.

"Where do you find yourself?" Her question breaks through the "silence," the screaming voices in my head.

"Lost." Tears well in my eyes.

"Do you enjoy that place?" She asks with a smile.

How can she smile at a question like that, when I experience such pain in my heart?

"No. I hate it."

"Then why do you stay there?"

"I have no choice."

"Really?" Her eyes are quite serious now.

"Elise, you must choose to stay in the pain if that is where you find yourself."

I feel judged and defensive. Cursing my cowardice legs, I long to get up from the table, run upstairs, throw my things into my suitcase and escape this place. For a long minute, I consider returning to New York. If I just operate "as if" everything is alright, it will eventually work itself out and actually "be" alright.

"Are you a victim, Elise?"

"I don't know. I don't want to be. But, look at this life. I didn't choose it! It was chosen for me." Tears are streaming down my cheeks now.

"Try on, for just a minute, that perhaps you *do* choose to be a victim."

"Who would choose that? No way. My mother always played the victim card. That's not me. I'm not going to be a victim. I just want my life back."

Dai-en smiles.

"We can't be a victim unless we accept that we are a victim."

"I don't understand," I admit.

"Listen, there is a pull for the ego to survive. Emotional pain from our past needs to renew itself, through experiencing more pain, in order to survive. Sometimes the pain we have experienced is the mode through which we prove our 'rightness' over another person. Simply, we were right and they were wrong, and the pain that they caused, that we now feel, proves this. Our pain is our evidence."

My blank stare pleads with Dai-en across the table to continue, to say something to bring some peace to my heart, not to leave me with simply pain and blame.

"What happened to you, in your childhood, to cause you to experience yourself as a victim?"

"I don't know. My father dying?"

"How old were you?"

"7."

"And what did you make that mean for you?"

I pause for a minute to think about her question.

"That I had done something to deserve it; that people who loved me would leave me." Dai-en's eyes soften, as she takes a deep breath, seeming to exhale for me. It feels good to cry, but it doesn't feel good to admit these things.

"Sounds pretty rough."

"Yeah, it was. I felt like he abandoned us. Or like G-d was punishing us. We were all alone."

"The impact that had on your life must have been profound."

"My mother suddenly had to do everything on her own. She went back to work. I went to a babysitter. I don't even know what happened in my brother's life. I guess he went to school."

"Elise, consider that you experienced yourself as a victim from that time. Consider that some of your responses to love and loss have been those of a 7 year old."

"But I'm not 7 anymore."

"Yes, that's true, but you never resolved what happened. You made it mean that you had done something wrong, that if you had acted differently, the outcome would have been different. You said that you weren't good enough, like it was your fault."

"Oh, I know it wasn't my fault."

"Of course, at 47 you know that it wasn't your fault, but your 7 year old self experienced it as having something to do with you. And you've been living out that story ever since, trying to gain control over the things that happen, over others and the choices they make."

"Hmm. You know that makes more sense than I care to admit. I always assumed Alan was going to leave ... eventually."

"You know you derive some benefit from believing that, and ultimately from that becoming a reality."

"Benefit? What do you mean?"

"You tell me. What do you 'get' from a man leaving you?"

31

"Get? Sadness, loneliness."

"Ok, yes, but I mean you get something quote-end-quote 'good.' What is it?"

"Good?" She must be crazy. How do I derive something good from the feeling of devastation and abandonment?

"Well, you've said you expected it. You get to be right about that. You get to be right about your father's death."

"I get to be right about him leaving, about me not being good enough."

"Exactly. And you get to be the victim."

"But I don't want that!"

"Elise, I think on some level, you do." We sit staring at each other for a long time. Finally, tears well up in my eyes and I begin to choke as if I have been crying for hours. It is coming out of me and I cannot stop it. How can I be willing to accept myself as a victim? I have tried my whole life to avoid this.

"What do you get from being a victim?"

I fidget in my seat. I can't get comfortable. Why are these kitchen chairs so hard?

"I can't think of anything but sadness and pain."

"It's hard to think about, Elise, I get it, but do you get something that appears beneficial? Empathy, attention, being right about men?"

"Sure, I guess I get all of that." I sit for a minute staring at a black smudge on the wall.

"Wow, this doesn't feel good."

Dai-en smiles. "Most people pass through life without ever getting any awareness around how they see themselves and why. Elise, this is heavy lifting.

What do you lose by being the victim and by not trusting others?"

"That's easy. I lose love and connection and togetherness. But those are the things I want."

"Exactly. Do you get it now?"

"Yeah, but I've existed like this for so long. I don't know if I can change."

"Tell me why you doubt whether you can change. What are you experiencing right now?"

"I honestly feel like my life would end if I gave this up. I so identify with being a victim; I truly see myself that way, even though I don't want to. If I'm not a victim, who am I?"

"I don't know. Why don't you tell me who you think you are? If you didn't have to be the victim any longer, who would you choose to be?"

I am the one who starts to smile now. I am grateful for this dinner, my kind friend, and her courage to be honest with me. My head is spinning in overwhelm. I'm not sure if I completely understand, and I'm confused by the appearance of a smile on my lips. I fear losing this moment, this feeling of release; I fear forgetting what she has said, and losing this brief glimmer of freedom.

CHAPTER FIVE

SUSQUEHANNA RIVER VALLEY, PENNSYLVANIA
MAY, 2012

Zucchini blossoms appear under umbrella-like leaves. The days are long; the afternoons are hot. The evening showers are a blessing. The yearlings have learned to fly and a letter arrives from Japan. After dinner, Dai-en composes a simple letter to Elise.

> My Dear Friend,
> Your presence is greatly missed. The garden is in full bloom following your visit.
> The Shakkei Temple in Chiba awaits your arrival. Please let me know when you can visit. Nishida-sensei hopes you can stay for at least one month.
> Loving peace,
> Dai-en

Three days later, in my apartment in Manhattan, I look up from the envelope in my hand with a smile across my face, and fear consuming my belly from the inside out. My head immediately fills with all of the reasons why I cannot go. I will abandon William when he needs me the most. I will lose William to a new life that his father is creating. Resolved, I decide to write to Dai-en, to express her appreciation but to let her know that I cannot possibly go at this time.

CHAPTER SIX

THE HAMPTONS, LONG ISLAND, NEW YORK
SEPTEMBER, 2012

The chill in the air after dusk indicates one thing: the anticipation of Fall. William's classes began two weeks ago and my house is once again silenced. The quiet is my curse these days. It fills my head with voices of doubt and fear. I am a pawn of the G-ds; fate assures my solitude and fear. I imagine a laughing king, sitting drunk on his throne, entertained by the twists in the story told by the raconteur. The jester's movements exaggerate the already unbearable drama of my life. Alan and I dance around each other. He silently creeps around our house, our life, my world. Like a coward he kowtows to me, subjugates himself to my every want, pretending these gestures will erase his actions and prove his love to me. The only thing it proves is who he is capable of being. I believe he never loved me; he couldn't have loved me if he destroyed our life this way. He single-handedly obliterated the landscape of the world we built together. He opened fire on our marriage, on William, and on me, without any regard for where his bullets fell. Surely there were moments when he prayed some of them would be direct hits and release him from the life that bound him tightly.

Shortly after returning from Dai-en's farm, we resolved to go to marriage therapy. We started going on "dates."

Many days I think of my conversation with Dai-en the last evening before I returned to the city. I am aware of my victim story. I recognize the attention and empathy I derive in seeing myself this way and telling others of how I have been wronged by Alan, yet still I am unable to figure out what all of this means for me.

Some days, anger overtakes me and I try on my suit of victim armor, stare at my reflection in the full length mirror on the back of our closet door, and loathe myself. In some odd way, it feels good to blame myself for all of this. It allows me to keep Alan perfect in my mind. This self-blame allows me to be right in choosing a good man, in doing the best I could. For moments I can consider an easier path, that of the martyr. If I remain the victim, I can say that I had nothing to do with our marriage ending.

As I daydream this fantasy into reality, I notice the wrinkled lines that sculpt my eyes, the toneless legs that seem so imperfect, the gravity-stricken breasts that seek the earth below, and I become aware of how much I hate the image reflected in the mirror. Crying, I begin to hit my thighs as I crumple to the carpet below, knowing that I cannot continue this way. I cannot act "as if" any longer. I can taste my imminent death in the salt of my tears, and I am profoundly aware that this cannot go on.

CHAPTER SEVEN

NEW YORK CITY
OCTOBER, 2012

The burnt coffee sits stagnant in its cradle marking mid-morning. The drops encircling the rim of my cup have dried like a watercolor painting left incomplete on the easel. Sitting still in *zazen* used to be a source of peace and provide some gesture at hope. Now, the voices of doubt in my head invade my morning. Credit cards bills, cell phone records, and money missing ... my rampage begins, as I start to tear our home apart. I look everywhere for evidence as to why and how my marriage is ending.

I fall to the floor of his office, like the strewn clothes of lovers. My open hands cradle my face, lying fetal, rocking back and forth, bent over, embracing my knees. Alan just stands over me watching. After a minute, I look up at him. I am a crazed woman, a lunatic. How will he ever love me? Look at me! I have lost it. I must look completely mad.

"Elise, come on." He drops down to his knees and awkwardly reaches towards me. An obligatory hand touches my shoulder. I shrug him away.

"Don't, please." My lip curls, as I struggle to speak through tears. "Please....don't...touch me." Angry words melt to tears of desperation. My hands catch the liquid that drips from my nose. Tears fall uncontrollably. What I don't realize at that moment, is that it is myself whom I hate. By believing something would change, I have betrayed myself.

"Elise, it's not what you think."

I look up at him, wiping the wetness on my now baggy jeans.

"You can't even look me in my eyes. You hate me."

"I don't hate you, Elise. I love you…"

He is silent. His eyes look back at mine, filled with tears. How dare he actually have tears in his eyes.

I stop crying. I just look across at him in utter disbelief. How is our marriage ending?

"I hate you." I want to hurt him with my words. I want him to feel pain slice through his heart the way I have. Instead, I am the pathetic one crying in the middle of the floor. Alan leans over me, hugging me. Blood from my finger drips onto the floor.

"Oh my G-d. How did you do that? Let me get you a band-aid." He gets up and leaves to our medicine cabinet. I look down. I must have cut my finger on my ring when I slammed my fist down. The band slides off easily from the wetness on my hand.

Alan returns and begins bandaging my finger.

"Elise, look at you. Come on. I just need some time. You are my north star, my beacon of light. Maybe it's not you. It's me. Just give me a bit of time. I am like a captain lost at sea, and you will guide me back home." He pauses for a moment, anticipating a response. I cannot look into his eyes. I stay buried in his shoulder, not for comfort, but to avoid this reality. I wish my eyes would close forever to this world. I long to have my existence melt into the horizon with the setting sun. The blood from my veins, the beating of my heart, the energy of my thoughts could melt into the vibrant colors and fade to black.

"I need you to be strong for both of us when I cannot be. I am lost, but I will find my way. Please, Elise, you are the northstar that will lead me back to our family."

How does his begging become meaningful to me? Why do his words continue to matter? I believe him. I begin to believe that he thinks I am strong and that I will be the hero in all of this. I will save our marriage. I will stand still long enough for him to find his way back to me. Commitment in marriage is not proven on wedding days. I understand that marriage is not about eating bon-bons and making love at the end of romantic dinners. This is the time for me to prove my commitment to him, to William, and to our family. I convince myself that I can do this. I will be more understanding and patient; I will be here for him when he realizes he does want our family.

In the next month, my investment in him and in our marriage, results in his further withdrawl. I become obsessed with his every action, and my spirit is frail. By the end of November, I realize I cannot continue to live like this, and I ask him to leave. By the first of December, I am writing to Dai-en to beg the opportunity to still go to Japan.

CHAPTER EIGHT

MANHATTAN, NEW YORK
JANUARY, 2013

We are sitting in the bar at the Mandarin. He orders me a drink without asking – extra dirty martini.

"You're trying to get me drunk?"

"A little hangover won't help you sleep on the plane tomorrow?"

"It might. I have a book packed I've been wanting to read."

"Yeah?"

Silence between us feels awkward now. I am overwhelmed by how strange it feels to sit across from the man I have shared so much with, and to feel like I do not know him. I take a long draw on my martini and feel the alcohol surge through my veins immediately.

"Listen, Elise. I have something I need to give you." He pushes a manila envelope across the table. My heart stops and I immediately start to shake. I curse the long stem of the martini glass realizing I will not get the funnel up to my lips again without spilling down the front of my silk blouse. Couldn't he have at least waited until my drink was half gone?

"Alan, not now. Not here."

"I'm sorry, Elise. But you're leaving tomorrow. I have to give these to you now."

"Does William know?"

"Of course not."

"I won't even have a chance to talk with him. I feel so sad for him. Do you even care about him anymore?"

"Come on, Elise. This has nothing to do with him. This is about us."

"Yes, but he is the one who suffers. Look what my life was like?"

"Elise, your life was not so bad. Come on. William will be fine. He doesn't even notice us anymore. He's into his friends and music. Kids are resilient."

"Alan, it's like you don't even know him. He's so withdrawn over all of this. He needs you now more than ever."

"Elise, he isn't losing me. I will always take care of you guys."

"It's not the same thing, Alan." The coveted olives sit in the bottom of my glass untouched. "So, that's it. It's over. The contents of our marriage dumped into a single envelope?"

"Come on, Elise. Why do you always have to be so dramatic? Look at you. You're moving on. Have an incredible trip. You finally get to go back to the place you have wanted to go all of these years. You'll be fine. I don't worry about you."

The seven year old girl, sits across the table in front of a half drained martini glass, and says, "You never did."

Chapter Nine

JFK Airport, New York
January, 2013

My mother said that when I was a little girl I always fell in the water when we went to the ocean or stopped by a lake. Even in November, when we drove east to the tiny twelve miles of coastline in New Hampshire to remember the summer past, climbing on the rocks with my older brother, I would inevitably end up soaked to my waist. Knowing my mother, it was not possible that her neglect was partial cause for my wintertime swim. I just sought to jump between two rocks, too far apart, too many times, and chance got the best of me and my dry clothes. I remember more than one occasion driving home wrapped naked in the red and black plaid, wool blanket we always had in the back of our station wagon.

Years later wrapped in a blue wool blanket in Akira's apartment waiting for the bath to fill, I remembered the warmth of sitting in the car with my brother and my mom driving home in the late afternoon, salty air on our skin and in our hair. She never got mad. She just hugged me. I miss my mother's arms, yet I know I can never go back to those seemingly perfect moments. No matter how much I long to feel the way I did at age eight when my mom held me and told me everything was going to be alright, I can never quite capture that feeling again.

Even when I was living in Asia in my twenties, I would get on a plane seeking my mother's arms. And when I was finally home I would sit with her on the couch sipping tea and talking. When the leaves had chilled at the bottoms of our cups, I nestled into the small of her arm in silence and pretended I was still small. That time was different though, for there was a constant looming knowledge that, however precious the moment was, in a couple days' time, I would get on a plane and return to the world I was seeking to create for myself, one that sought love and success and adventure.

As much as my mother wished those things for me, they were not things she could give me, like that warm woolen blanket in the back of her car. She knew in her heart that she had to send me away in order for me to find my own place in the world.

Now, as I stand with clear glass separating me from my own little angel, I understand the perceived feelings of my mother. I am departing for Japan. William is only fifteen and I am choosing to leave him, in search of my own sanity, a gift I must bring back for both of us. Our rendezvous will be more than a month from now; I cannot yet imagine how I will bear the distance and face the fear of loss in my belly.

We take for granted the millions of genetic failures that can occur with any pregnancy, but as I stand here I feel again the thousands of things that can go wrong with the flight, my journey, his time without me. One wrong turn, one oversight, and my precious son's life and my relationship to him, could suddenly be at stake. At this moment, everything feels so vulnerable and tentative. Leaving him feels wrong.

As I approach the check-in counter behind the glass, I search my rationale, with desperation, for one good reason to go. My sadness and fear of leaving William temporarily overshadow the loss I am experiencing at the end of my marriage. These feelings nearly paralyze me, nearly prevent me from embarking on this journey which might restore my ability to parent, to feel human again, and to once again be present in his life.

As I take my boarding pass from the agent, I am wrapped up in all of the reasons to stay. As I hand my pass to the agent at the door, I remember my son's first day of school – he embraced me and then skipped off, with a smile that a mom prays for, to join his friends in the schoolyard. I sobbed uncontrollably the entire way to the grocery store. As I walked into our house after an hour of shopping, I cursed the silence that echoed my tears.

As the gate closes and the plane backs up to the runway, I place my hand onto the glassed window next to me to silently reach one more time for reasons to stop the flight from taking off.

My insatiable love for William has fueled my tiny desire to continue living during the last months. I will seek you, my child, I will bear you. I will rear you. I will watch you. I will smile to you – even when you do not realize I am watching. I will hold you. I will kiss your soft forehead and gently stroke your flawless hair. I will let you go. I will long for you ... and, I will do all of these things in silence ... except for my tears – the sound of each drop will resonate across the mountains, oceans and deserts of time. I will wait an eternity for you ... and then, I will wait for you again.

I pull my hand away from the window and turn towards the dark cabin. Emptiness fills my chest. My mind longs for my son; my soul feels the loss of a lover.

I feel pressure on my chest as the plane ascends to the heavens. I look out into the darkness that blankets the ocean below me. The bodies of water that surround us both isolate and connect us. For a moment I curse the vast water before me. For decades now it has taken me away from loved ones, but it has also brought me back. Defying science, I swear the oceans are salty for the centuries of tears cried into them.

Today I cry for all loves lost. This separation from my son embodies my fears realized. I blame Alan for all of the loss, fear, and loneliness I feel, while I also blame him for most of the joy, love and pride I have experienced for the last decade and a half. Neither assessment is fair, but today that is how I feel.

I close my eyes and imagine his arms around me from behind. They shelter me from the reality I face. His breath whispers something in her ear.

"He'll be back and I love you."

I turn to see Alan. He sits beside me to the right, the direction from which the wind is blowing into my face.

He smiles; I snuggle into the crux of his arm and place my head on his shoulder. He always does this; he will not let me feel alone. William left this morning for a week of camp in rural Vermont.

"I'm glad you're here."

"It's the only place to be."

I smile; I love him. He saves me from myself. Only temporarily, he takes away all of the reasons for my fears.

45

I wake from a fitful sleep, cheeks wet with the knowledge that I am alone. How am I going to live without him? I have no idea how I am going to find a way to live without Alan.

CHAPTER TEN

CHIBA, JAPAN
JANUARY, 2013

The express train stops at South Chiba station. As the doors open I feel the cold lash of winter against my cheeks. An odd sense of home strikes me as I stand on the busy platform. I look in either direction and as far as the eye can see there are businessmen and students waiting, walking, moving toward their morning destinations. I have been here before and yet it is my first time to stand at this station. I have returned to Japan after more than two decades. Nine months of sitting *zazen* told me that it was time for me to meet my second love again, alone, to face what I have not allowed myself to feel for so many years. A letter sent, a response anticipated and received – all of the details were arranged – simply, that I was expected in early January in Chiba. I was to return to Japan, this time not as a recent college graduate seeking adventure and employment, but as a woman lacking identity, feeling abandoned and alone. I have returned to attempt to fill a void in my heart which has long existed, even before the dissolution of my marriage.

I have come to Japan again to intersect a parallel world from which I diverted many years ago. My life has been filled with a husband, a son, travel, extended family, love, many joys and deep sorrows. The life that I chose so many years ago delivered on its promises of adventure, heart strings, and connections. Years ago living in the countryside of northern Japan, I felt such aloneness, a solitude that delivers inner quietude, time for personal growth – scholarly, physical, spiritual. And after years of isolating my heart from hurt, I decided to return to the United States to reunite with my family, my country, myself. In many ways, I first ran to Japan to leave behind the hurts of childhood and young love. I then escaped to Hong Kong and other parts of Asia, seeking love and fulfillment. My return to the United States marked a certain defeat in my life. I had not found what I sought, and I longed to be near those whom I believed loved me the most.

Over the years my life became filled with the man whom I believed to be my soul mate, our family, and our child. My world became meaningful in the traditional sense, defined by my relationships, and slowly my solitary world was silenced. It is true that my life became happier but it is also true to say that my life became less peaceful. I had all of the things that one seeks – a spouse, a beautiful child, caring families, wealth, time to vacation – but I no longer had an inner world where I defined myself in the singular.

Over the years, my identity has been marked by my giving. In pledging my heart, I became a wife; in giving birth, I became a mother; in caring for aging parents, I expressed what it was to be a daughter. I return to Japan to embrace my singularity, to face my husband's departure from our marriage, to realize the finality of all life, and to remember what filled the quiet spaces in my mind so many years ago. In leaving the comfort of home, I have returned to my second country, the one I have had a quiet, secret affair with over the years.

The train doors close behind me and the morning bustle is silenced. The platform is nearly empty now and my feet start moving towards the stairs as though they have nothing else to do. I feel a chill on my forehead from the cold sweat under my simple clothes. My pack is heavy; surely I will look silly arriving at the temple with so much. Years of packing for many have left me unable to travel lightly.

The night before I left for Japan, my entire upper west side neighborhood stood in pitch black from a wind storm. I basked in the quiet smell of wax burning in the candles around my apartment. I sat sipping wine remembering the childhood nights when our electricity was downed by a similar wind storm up the New England coast. My mother, brother and I sat together on our bean bags in the doorway between our family room and kitchen, talking, teasing, and laughing. Moments like that were the most "family" times I can remember. Sitting together, I secretly prayed the electricity would stay out forever and that the morning sun would not rise; I longed to sit lovingly together always, to evade our cluttered world of struggle and emotions and disappointment. When the power was restored, we scattered to opposite corners of our little house to resume co-habitation. Perhaps it was those times that have led me to welcome slight tragedy, to covet the closeness that only misfortune can bring. Until recently, I have had the habit of daydreaming to imagine what chain of events would occur if disaster hit my perfect life. Who would come to the rescue? What would they do to console the tragic? How long would the closeness stay? These masochistic daydreams stopped abruptly when Alan revealed to me his desire to spend the second half of his life without me. At the

49

very moment he uttered his words, regret flooded into my eyes, realizing all of the wasted moments I had spent longing for the dramatic. My silent, frivolous prayers answered, when all along I had not realized anyone had been listening.

I go through the turnstile and exit the station in front of the taxi stand. Years ago arriving at the bullet train *shinkansen* platform in Niigata, I was welcomed by a large group of teachers and students holding embarrassingly large banners written in broken English – Welcome Miss Teacher Elise – Our Happy Teacher – Nishi School Happy Day. Today buses spill soot into the air and the smell of fresh baked bread fills my nostrils. The "early January arrival" is so surprisingly open and loose for the punctual, planned Japan that I once knew. I know little of what to expect of temple life, but one thing I understand is that absolute time is relative behind the weathered wooden gate through which I will pass. My arrival is incidental, my journey is tentative and my usefulness is uncertain. It is not that my host has low expectations of me, but rather that he has no expectations at all. His offer to "host" me is an act of charity, a demonstration of mercy, a month of grace, to save me from myself.

I am looking for Higashi Street. I follow the taxi round-about to the main road to read the sign. My right shoulder is tight under the weight of my pack. I can hear my breath and feel the burn of the cold air in my lungs. I have to cross the street to see the sign. I do not recognize the simple characters for "east" and "street" as I approach the sign and I realize the ten minute hike has been in vain. I have exited the station on the wrong side. Because of the elaborate rail system in this part of the country, simply walking around to the other side of the station is impossible. I turn back, face the station, look up to the three story metal monstrosity before me and realize there is no other way. Across the street, around the round-about, into the station, a long, misunderstood, broken explanation to the uniformed man at the ticket turnstile, the escalator up, the walk along the platform, stairs down, another explanation at the other side as to why I do not have a ticket, finally I emerge at the other side.

This side of the station is much busier -- buses spewing black clouds of diesel exhaust, a manned taxi stand with noisy whistles blowing, several kiosks selling magazines and *manga* comics, gum and cigarettes. Somehow the other side of the station seemed slightly more fitting for a temple setting. I decide to ask this time. Yes, Higashi Street is straight ahead. The sweet smell of frying dough fills the air as I walk past Mister Donut. I remember afternoons inside scoffing down three or four pastries with weak "American" coffee just to get a familiar glimpse of the taste of home. The sweet bean versions were my favorite. This was my life – a bridge between two cultures, two tastes of life: sweet bean donuts, pizza with tuna and corn, hamburgers served open face with Japanese "basil" *shiso* leaf, white radish *daikon* and soy sauce. I suspect that this journey will be devoid of such cultural intersections. This time, I stand before a dynamic country with such a bustling pace, asking for basic flavors and the monotony of a simple lifestyle.

Numerous turns and several inquiries later, I arrive outside of large wooden gates. I touch the splintering timber and the smell of tar fills my nose. My eyes follow the heavy doors to the place where they intersect the blue sky. A few tiny abandoned

51

snowflakes fall to my cheeks. I squint at the light above and breathe deeply. I have arrived. In some ways my journey has ended and I feel relief, yet I know the most difficult journey is soon to begin. A single tear falls down my right cheek and I taste salt. I miss Alan. I always have envisioned this moment with him by my side or at the very least across the ocean waiting for me. My eyes fall with the realization that I am utterly alone. It does not matter where I stand in this world today, there is no one beside me. Any trace of the warmth of the body which stood beside me for nearly two decades is gone. A single heart is beating inside of this cavity I call my body, and it echoes down a lonely canyon. I curse the lack of gratitude I lived for so many years of my marriage. I curse the perfection I sought and consistently eluded. Running with such conviction in one direction led me to a narrow path where only one can fit.

There are two smaller doors to either side of the gate. The iron handle on the one to the right is worn shiny from use and I reach out and push the door open. I step into a large pebbled courtyard that leads up to the main temple hall. A shaven monk is busily sweeping the top steps of the temple hall. I can see the steamy air flowing upwards from his heavy breathing. His actions are swift and deliberate, skilled movements, a product of repetition. I begin to walk towards the purification fountain to wash my hands and rinse my mouth. I am startled by the loud crunch under my feet; the sweeping monk does not hesitate, never lifting his head to acknowledge me. The cold water falls from the wooden ladle and strikes my hands in gloves of ice. I feel the liquid warm in my mouth, clumsily spit the water in the drain basin below, and wipe my dripping mouth on my sleeve. I approach the steps and try to remember whether to remove my shoes at the bottom of the steps or at the top before entering the hall. A compromise – I take them in my hand so as not to insult the working monk, carry them up the stairs, remove my backpack, and leave everything outside.

Walking into the temple hall, I smell musky incense, sit *zazen* style on the *tatami* to the side and decide to wait. Silence. Emptiness. I sit for twenty minutes, one hour, more. My legs are numb; my stomach is peevish. I am not expected today or on any specific day. I decide to sit until I am noticed.

My head fills quickly with judgment, anger, and great sorrow. The whirlwind that captured my life nine months ago prevents me from finding stable ground. When he withdraws, I find myself dismissing our marriage in anger. During the times when he draws me closer in sentimentality, I long for simpler times and feel hope for our marriage. One week he calls me his beacon of light that will carry him from his darkness; another week he convinces me that we are not right for each other. "Maybe we never wanted the same things," he concludes sitting at the far end of our nine foot sofa. From where I "spin," it is clear to me that his actions are those of a man who longs to be single. His words refute this desire, at times, but finally I find myself in the same place – alone.

For a man who wanted me and our marriage so much in late November, it did not take long for the divorce petition to find its way to our hotel cocktail table in early January. Perhaps it was his last ditch effort to get me to cancel my trip to Japan. It was his attempt to control me and prevent my time to heal. I filed for an extension until I return, he agreed reluctantly. I left him our son, like collateral, to care for. When I think of William, my stifled breath shallows further, and I feel light headed. In the last nine months, I have lost twenty-two pounds, my capacity to sleep, and my ability to be present in my son's life. I know in my heart that this time in Japan is a matter of life and death, but being away from William feels unbearable and scary.

CHAPTER ELEVEN

SHAKKEI TEMPLE, CHIBA, JAPAN
JANUARY, 2013

I have fallen to sleep. The soreness at the base of my neck wakes me. My stomach has given up and quieted. Looking back towards the open door, I notice that the sky has begun to darken. Piercing silence, the temple bell is struck somewhere and I hear a shuffling noise like a duffle bag being dragged down a wooden hall. Two black figures hurl the heavy wooden doors shut and a dozen or so monks file into the main *tatami* section before the Shakyamuni Buddha. I am chilled until the newly lit incense seems to fill the air with warmth. Silence. One monk stands, facing away from the others towards the front of the room. A chant echoes from his mouth, the others follow with whispered voices. A cloud of steam rises from the group and I realize the temperature in the room is the same as outside. Cold.

Sudden silence falls; open hands rest on folded legs, each pair the same as the next. My eyes fall easily on the floor before me. My awkwardness distracts me from the task at hand. I find it difficult to quiet my insecure, anticipating mind. Will I be noticed? Fear wallows up inside of me. Exactly twenty minutes pass until a single monk rises to strike the bell inside the hall. The group rises uniformly and with great ease even for those who have been sitting *zazen* for such a long time.

Is the assured pain in their legs ignored or unnoticed from training? I pray to learn in time.

In another minute, the hall is emptied and I am alone again. The reverberating sound of deliberate footsteps on wood makes me look up.

"Excuse me, will you join us for dinner?"

I follow him across the room and into a side hallway. The corridor is long and very dark; when we are halfway to what appears to be the end, I remember my backpack and shoes outside the temple hall and wonder if I should have left them. The exuding silence stops me from attempting to say anything. We enter an unexpected door on the right and I slide the paper screen *shoji* door shut behind me. Following my leader, I fill a bowl with rice, place pickles on my wooden tray, and carefully take up a steaming bowl of clear soup. I find a single empty *zabuton* sitting pillow, already placed in expectation of my partaking in this meal. Before me lay a single pair of disposable chopsticks wrapped in simple white paper, like those found in any restaurant across Japan. Each of the monks has a pair of chopsticks that belong to the temple, but I am still a guest. No eyes have risen to greet me; there is absolutely no acknowledgement of my presence, yet, the second I sit, every monk raises his chopsticks and begins to eat. The meal is finished within two minutes but the monks quietly sip tea until somehow the group knows when I have placed the last grain of rice from my bowl in my mouth, and at that exact moment, everyone stands. A whirlwind of deliberate activity surrounds me, restoring the room to order. I feel completely helpless. Like an orchestra, each person knows what to do to clean the room. Trays and bowls are stacked and hurried off to an invisible kitchen.

Zabuton are stacked neatly in the corner. The table is wiped; the floors are swept. Acting in unison, everyone finishes their job at exactly the same time and leaves the room. I walk to the open *shoji* door and find my backpack just outside. Who brought it to me so quickly? Did he forsake a meal to clean up after me? My shoes are wrapped inside a small, draw stringed bag set next to my pack.

"Will you be spending the night?"

"Yes, please, if it is alright."

I am led further down the hall which abruptly turns to the right. Near the end, I am led to a *shoji* door on the left.

"The futon is in the closet. The women's bath is down the hall behind the red *noren* hanging curtain. Please shut the light by 8:00 promptly."

"Thank you. *Yoroshiku onegaishimasu.*"

I enter the room and place my backpack in the corner. I remove the futon from the closet and lay it in the center of the room. I take my pajamas and simple slippers out of my pack. I place the slippers outside my door. My toes feel like ice as I pull off my socks and for a minute I curse the burn I anticipate in entering the heat of the bath at the end of the hall.

I am alone in the bath and realize others might be waiting. A guest would be allowed to bathe first, alone, even if others might follow together in a small group. As my footsteps find their way down the hall returning to my room, I hear the faint sound of feet entering through the *noren* behind me. Chilled by the short walk, I quickly close the light and climb under the thin blanket covering the futon. Great relief sends my body to sleep. For the first time in a very long time, I feel home.

CHAPTER TWELVE

SHAKKEI TEMPLE, CHIBA, JAPAN
JANUARY, 2013

I wake to the smell of fire. We are standing outside on the curb in front of our lawn staring back at our house as it melts before us in flames. An overwhelming feeling of gratitude fills my tears — no lives lost. In the months of denial and anger that follow, I try to remember this gratitude and fail. A misplaced wire found its purpose: to destroy our memories, to melt my son's bronzed baby shoes, and erase our lives.

Photographs, diplomas, art collected from travels around the world — everything is blown into the wind like urned ashes tossed from a mountainside. Only these ashes were not willed. As we stand there my husband vows never again to live in a home he has not built himself. We will find land, a new space, and slowly we will rebuild our memories. We walk through the black soot looking for any signs of our" previous" lives. We find melted balls of precious metals and singed corners of pages. A burnt piece of my son's blue teddy bear that Alan won at the fair years before makes me burst into tears. I am unable to move. Black tears streak down my cheeks. Wiping my face, I inadvertently draw lines down my face like a warrior preparing for battle.

We collect photographs from family and friends. We fill in the missing pieces; our lives are no longer linear but a collage of things collected and found.

I wake to the smell of fire with tears in my eyes. At first, I am unable to comprehend where the tears on

58

are from. The room is dark so I stand and slide the *shoji* window open. I notice the left corner of the paper is torn and stained. Peering through the opening, I look but there is no fire in sight.

Lying back on my futon, I slowly remember my dream and the day I thought all of our memories had burned. Until now, I believed that was the pivotal moment in my life of rebuild. Somehow the material loss seems so incidental now. I think for a moment of my inability to collect missing pieces from those whom I love. There is no one who can give me Alan, our family intact, or my marriage. Most of these memories will simply become individual pictures in the collage of my life. The hopes and dreams that have burned into the past will have to be replaced with new, different ones. Like our material losses of that day, some pictures and memorabilia will be gone forever. I see at this moment that new memories will be created over time. Some of the things we replaced after the fire, I liked better than the old. While other cherishables, like the pottery my grandmother made before she died, are gone forever replaced only by a longing.

Part of life is learning what we will have to live without. Today, however, I recognize that both what we have, and what we have either lost or long for, are only a part of what we currently know exists. There is also an entire universe comprised of that which we don't even know exists – possibility, potentiality, creation. We have to create the possibility of something entirely new for transformation to actually occur. Destruction and loss are part of change; nothingness and creation are part of transformation. One must have nothingness in order to experience creation, for we do not know what we do not know.

With the sky just barely gesturing towards dawn, I carry my shoes back down the long corridor that leads to the main hall. Finding a door to the back garden, I walk along the long building to survey the number of windows. Before long, I am walking back towards Higashi Street. I pass a tea shop and find the source of my morning fire. Puffs of gray smoke rise from a metal tin where the shopkeeper is burning green leaves to make roasted *bancha* tea. The strong smell melts a smile on my lips and I bow slightly to the woman stirring the mix. Her skin is dark and wrinkled from years of hard work and tannin ash. I wonder if we share something; her gracious eyes tell me that we might. A few doors down I find a small store that sells *shoji* paper and glue. Later that morning, I will show the man the piece I have cut from the cedar frame. He will match it quickly but will be surprised to hear the quantity I require. After a few minutes he will return from the back and tell me that he can deliver everything that afternoon. Because of the quantity needed, some of the rice paper must be ordered and it will take until the end of the week. His fingers dance between the knobs of a wooden abacus and he gives me a price. I hand him a piece of paper on which the temple address is written. He suddenly stops and stares at me. A small laugh interrupts his lingering eyes.

"The Shakkei Temple?" he asks.

"Yes, please."

"Are you American?"

"Yes. I have come to stay at the temple for some time."

"You are working there?"

"I will study and work. Yes."

"Study Japanese?"

60

"Yes, perhaps. And to sit *zazen* meditation."

"Really? Ahh, that's difficult."

"Not more difficult than changing *shoji*." We laugh.

"This is true." He says still laughing. I can tell he wants to ask more, but perhaps is not sure where to begin. I finish the now cooled tea that his wife served me. Thanking him for his help, I pay cash and leave.

The paper and glue arrive before lunch.

"Excuse me. Are you Engle-san?" A knock at the door startles me. I have been sitting *zazen* in the center of my room, by myself, for a good part of the morning. The pains in my stomach are partially allayed by the prospect that I might be invited for lunch.

"Yes. I am sorry I didn't want to interrupt dinner last night. I have arrived yesterday from America and I am hoping to speak with Nishida-sensei."

"Oh. There is someone here from a shop in town with a delivery for you. Please follow me." I realize I have not been recognized yet as an expected visitor, but rather that my supplies have arrived from the *shoji* shop.

My messenger helps me to carry all of the paper back to my room. He leaves the supplies without question and disappears. Ten minutes later a young man arrives at my door and tells me that Nishida-sensei will be back in a few days. I show him the letter that Dai-en received from the temple inviting me to arrive in the early part of the year.

"Oh, Engle-san. Yes, yes. We are expecting you."

We are sitting on our knees facing each other and I bow deeply.

61

"Nice to meet you. I am Matsuda."

I bow again. "Nice to meet you."

The next week is spent repairing the *shoji*. I begin in my room and move down the hall, first in the direction of the bathrooms, and then in the other direction. I understand it is not the best place to begin, but I finish all of the students' rooms before I move onto the meditation hall, smaller study rooms, and dining facilities. It is hard work and my fingers begin to crack from the cold, dry air and the strong glue. I remain on the periphery of the temple students' lives but begin to notice slight bows from individuals who have appreciated the care I have shown to the temple grounds and to their windows. I feel grateful for the opportunity to contribute even though my hands are in shambles.

I am a guest at dinners still. There is a place that is regularly set for me but it is off to the side. I am not asked to join in meditations, but this is to be expected. I do not think that anyone else knows of my arrival, and until Nishida-sensei returns I will remain peripheral.

It is my eighth day at Shakkei Temple. I return to the *shoji* shop in the morning to order more supplies. The gentleman there informs me that the supplies will be charged to Matsuda-san at Shakkei Temple. This surprises me but I decide not to ask any questions, so as not to insult Matsuda-san or confuse my kind friend.

I am completely out of paper and my work cannot continue until the supplies arrive. One of the students in the room next to me is surprised when I ask him if I can help him this morning by cleaning the women's bathroom. He hesitates but understands that

I prefer to have work rather than sit in my room by myself. He agrees and I am grateful.

Later in the day, Matsuda-san comes to find me, asking to take me to meet with Nishida-sensei who has arrived the previous evening. I have been scrubbing the tiles on the floor of the *sento*. I ask for Matsuda-san to allow me five minutes to clean up. He agrees to return. My heart begins to pound immediately, at the anticipation of meeting Nishida-sensei, my dear friend Dai-en's teacher. Authority has always intimidated me. Somehow I must make the transition from bathroom cleaner to student of Dai-en in minutes. Japanese phrases run through my head at nano-speed. I place the strong, bristled brushes in my bucket, quickly rinse the floor with the shower head and return to my room. In my head, I debate whether to show humility by wearing street garments or show commitment by donning the simple work cloak of the temple which I have borrowed from my first friend. I choose the latter. When Matsuda-san returns I am kneeling on the *tatami* mat by my door waiting.

"Engle-san."

"Yes." I follow in silence.

We walk down a long series of wooden hallways. I notice the wood framing the *shoji* rice paper has changed slightly; it is darker and slightly shinier. Later I will learn that this is the "older" part of the temple. Nishida-sensei resides in this section and has a simple inner-office there. The aged smell of incense seems to have permanently altered this area of the temple. Shakkei Temple was built in the 10th century as a first outpost for the Shingon sect of Zen. Incense has burned in these halls for over one thousand years. I am humbled by my mere 46 years.

"Shitsurei shimasu." I speak again the words I first uttered entering the teachers' room at Nishi Junior High School in northern Japan decades ago to humbly apologize should my arrival interrupt anyone's work. Not sure now whether these same words are appropriate, I have faith that Nishida-sensei will understand my intentions.

His outstretched palm points toward a single *zabuton* pillow sitting before his low resting *kotatsu*-style, covered wooden desk.

"Sumimasen." I first kneel on the floor before the pillow and slowly touch my head to the *tatami*. Dai-en had coached me: express simple honor and humility; do not overdo it. Without further words I sit back on the *zabuton*. I quickly doubt whether the stance I have taken will endure a long conversation. Sitting lotus would have been a better choice but my initial hesitation to find a comfortable sitting position has ensured that I will have numb legs when I next try to stand up.

"Engle-san, welcome to Shakkei Temple. Dai-en-san tells me in her letter that she has known you for a very long time. We are happy to welcome one of her students."

I bow but remain silent, fearing I might interrupt.

"There is much work to be done at the temple. Please tell me how long you will be with us."

"If it is acceptable, I hope to stay for one month. I look forward to the work I might do here."

"I understand that you have already begun the project of changing the *shoji* here at the temple. Where did you learn to do this? It is not an easy task."

64

"When I was young, I lived in northern Japan and worked as an English teacher at a junior high school. I had a simple apartment and at the end of the year I was required to change the *shoji*."

"One time does not make an expert and I have seen your work."

"My husband and I built a Japanese style house near the beach in New York, and the *shoji* did not weather the salt air very well."

"Ahh, yes. I understand you are from New York City."

"Yes, but we have also lived on Long Island for many years while our son has been young."

"It is a blessing to have children. My children are the work of this temple. You must miss your family."

"Yes. My son is a high school student. I miss him very much. He is with his father."

Tea arrives and we sit in silence for some minutes. Nishida-sensei seems to be in deep thought.

"Please continue your work. If you need something, please tell me. Please join our colleagues in their daily routine of meditation and meals, if you wish."

"Yes, please. I will be most grateful for that opportunity."

"Engle-san, you have some experience meditating, don't you?"

"Yes, I have sat with Dai-en sensei for many years. We met when I was in college."

"Is that so? But you don't live next to her, do you?"

"Oh no. I live quite far. It is about 3 hours drive."

65

"So you have a daily practice then? You sit at your home?"

"Yes, most of the time, but sometimes it is very difficult."

"Ah, yes. Many good things are."

Nishida-sensei pauses for a few minutes. I anticipate that he is about to share something important with me, but instead I sit watching the curls of steam rise from his tea cup. I wonder if our meeting is over. It feels awkward and I want to leave.

"Well, you will meet with me here every two days, then. 10:00 a.m. after morning chores. Your time here is short." I am thinking he means the month I am meant to spend at Shakkei, but then he continues, "We each can transition at any time. You should not waste another minute." I realize he means our lives are short. Mine feels terribly long these days.

"I want you to write some stories for me."

"Stories?" I blurt out not pausing to consider what he might mean by this.

"Yes, stories about your life. I don't mean what has happened in your life – non-fiction, you call it? I want you to write the fiction stories."

I must look very confused, questioning whether I understand his Japanese correctly.

"I want you to write down briefly something that happened, that's the non-fiction part, and then I want you to write down, what you made that mean. For example, if a teacher told you that you were not a good student, that's what happened, but you deciding he was right, and that you were not as smart as the other children, and therefore not as good as the others, well that's what you made that mean. That's the fiction part. Do you understand?"

I say, "I do," but I realize that I don't really think I understand. I'm suddenly very nervous and confused.

"That's it, then, we start tomorrow."

"Thank you, Sensei, I am very grateful."

I quickly finish my tea, bow deeply again, walk backwards the short distance to the door, bow again and step out of the room. My legs are stiff and sore, even from the short conversation. Matsuda-san is waiting for me in the hallway. I smile to him and he returns me to my room. Twenty minutes later he comes to my room with a piece of paper that lists the daily schedule at the temple. There is also a short handbook riddled with broken English explaining the rules of the temple. I thank him. I already know that my next task will be mending the handbook's English. Thankfully, I have brought my laptop with me from New York.

CHAPTER THIRTEEN

SHAKKEI TEMPLE, CHIBA, JAPAN
JANUARY, 2013

Nishida-sensei has asked me to write stories about my life and I don't know where to begin. I feel embarrassed and exposed by each idea that comes into my head. I blamed Max for not marrying me in my early 20's. The other girls received fraternity pins and engagement rings, and revealed them at sisterhood candlelight ceremonies. I wasn't good enough. Richard left me on the beach of Sado Island, and didn't reach out again. For years I felt foolish about the connection I "imagined" we had. When I first returned to the United States, I found his phone number and called it. A woman answered and I never called again. Akira had an ex-wife, two daughters, and a girlfriend. I had 4 women to compete with in my mind, every encounter with him validated I wasn't the one. He had never even been out of Japan; the fantasy of him moving back to the States with me seems like a ridiculous premise now. I was constantly the unchosen one in his life. Every story I consider, has the same theme: me, insecure, needy, unable to truly "see" or acknowledge love when it was in front of me. I was never good enough, because if I had been, then the story about myself that defined my life, would not have been correct. I needed to not be good enough in order to be "right" and in order to predict and control that which scared me, the unknown. It seems insane to me now. I begin to write;

third person feels more comfortable for the "fiction" I am "creating."

Tokyo, Japan
September, 1993

She walks out of the front gate and closes the latch behind her. It is a short walk to the bike path that runs along the train tracks. She is living with a family in a western suburb of Tokyo. Shimmying between the metal barriers that prevent cars or motorcycles from entering the path, she begins to run. The first time she ran down this path, she only ran a couple of kilometers before turning around to head home. Over the months that follow she ventures further until one day the path passes the last station and opens up to a field.

She follows the path across the field and up a hill, winding around to the right and into a forest. The path suddenly diverts from the parallel road and into a dark, dense woods. The Indigo Girls blare in her ears. "Up On the Watershed." She runs up an embankment to her left just as the chorus of the song explodes, tears come to her eyes. Before her stands a huge, dammed reservoir. Thick trees border the vast water, reminding her of New England. The coincidental moment seems riddled with meaning. She is alone. She is stopped in her tracks with tears streaming down her face, wishing only that there was someone with whom to share this.

For weeks following this afternoon, she will try to remember what song she began her run with so she could attempt to repeat the beauty of this moment when song coincided with landscape so perfectly. Recapturing the moment motivates her. She soon finds the right place to begin her run and she repeats the scene again and again. After weeks of repetition, she encircles the lake, another five miles.

The lake becomes an inspiration to her. She begins to take a small pad and pen along with her in the kangaroo pouch of her anorak. She sits on the edge of the lake and writes poetry. Months later, after she meets Akira and their affection grows, she takes him to this place. They run together along the path for more than forty-five minutes before they arrive. Yes, he knows of the place. Yes, it is unexpected and special.

He introduces her to the small, wild flowers that grow around the area. Later, she returns there alone on bicycle with her camera to take photographs of their found treasures. She goes there to cry. She rewards herself with this place. When the snow begins to fall, she feels sadness and longs to sit in the sunshine on the shores again. She watches the ducks as they swim hard into the wind. Their little bodies work so hard, only to end up in the exact same place where they began. She thinks of what will happen if they do not swim as hard as they do against the wind. Their little bodies will remain huddled against the wind on the shore. The reservoir will freeze over along with their food source. She understands the importance of their hard work and knows that their stationery swim is not in vain. Her life is, at times, the same.

There are times when she seems to stay in one place no matter how hard she works for something or desires it. Her life and its efforts seem to be in vain. Her affection for people too, at times, seems to be in vain. She adores Akira, who has a very sick mother and an ex-wife. Yet, she cannot help herself. For the ducks, the wind will slow at the end of spring. In her own life, there will be times of ease ahead. She will reach the other shore; her life, her efforts, her love will be realized. Patience is her only choice. Longing is her constant curse.

She once went to the hospital with Akira to visit his mother and administer one of the three daily doses of Chinese herbs. It was already past 11:00 p.m. but the main hospital doors were still unlocked. They parked his station wagon in the fire lane in front of the doors. The hospital personnel were used to his routine.

They had been drinking at a local sushi bar and lost track of time and of the number of bottles they had opened. She followed him in silence. He knew the dark hallways better than his own home. He did not say as much, but he had wanted to share this part of his life with her for some time.

They entered the sterile room. The strong smell of Chinese herbs filled her nose, a stark contrast to the industrial clean smell of the hallway. He went to work. His mother lay motionless on the bed. He gently rubbed his hands from his mother's forehead to the back of her head. She was struck with the shine in his mother's hair and the beauty of her skin. He spoke quietly to her and held her hand. Her eyes did not open; her cheeks shown no smile; her limbs did not move. Years of lying flat had caused her muscles to atrophy.

Akira went to work preparing her medicines. Boiled water, steeping herbs, strained liquid, he filled sterile plastic syringes with the potions and held up her body, slowly injecting the liquids into her mouth. She swallowed deeply.

She had been in a coma for more than four years, following a stroke. She was a medical mystery: her brain activity was normal, her vitals stable, but she would not wake up. Her slender body looked so small on the big bed. She reached out to touch his mother's hand; it was warm and soft. She bowed her head in silent prayer.

Akira had refused her an I.V. She had no feeding tubes; her food was simply these precious herbs. Akira and his sister shared the feeding task; the private hospital had agreed to let her stay but would not administer the herbal medicines. He would not allow them to anyway. No one would care for her but her family; he had insisted. He fed her each morning on the way to work at his insurance office, his sister took the afternoon shift on her return home, and he came back every night.

71

His soft, strong hands rubbed her legs and gently massaged her feet. He tested her reflexes and her legs moved slightly. He covered her legs with the sheet and warm blankets. He turned her pillow and kissed her forehead. This struck her because Japanese do not often use this form of affection, especially not with adult family members. But Akira was a very loving man.

He picks her up on the corner next to her house early one morning. Her home-stay parents would not approve of their relationship. He is eighteen years older than she. He plays tennis with her home-stay parents who are sixty-nine and sixty-six. He hands her a warm mug of coffee from his thermos. They drive for twenty-minutes to another train line south of theirs. They park; it is not yet 6:30. The first Saturday train is waiting for them. His pack is heavier than hers; he always comes prepared. He buys their tickets and they ascend the stairs. He respects her strength and yet still finds ways to care for her. They step from the platform to the train; he takes her pack as she moves to sit down. They nestle close together. Within ten minutes a whistle blows, the doors close, and the train begins to move. Wet, green trees pass quickly outside of the window. From one sleepy town to the next, the cars move along stopping at every station. Other hikers find their place on the train; yellow and orange-red ponchos cover large packs and fall toward heavy, wet boots. The floor of the train is covered with wet footprints; the air is silent and damp.

At the next stop the doors open and they get off. They have to walk along the side of the road for about a kilometer. Akira has been there before. She wonders with whom. Their army green ponchos blend with the foliage but few cars are on the road this morning. He steps to the right up a short stack of stairs. She follows, reaching for his offered hand. The vertical ascent is surprisingly steep even for a mountainous hike. He catches her balance and sends her ahead. She finds a good stick to combat the spiders they are sure to encounter across the path.

72

"Here," he simply says. Her eyes follow his hand to a pale purple lady slipper standing in the rain. The green shiny leaves fold over into a natural water way for subsequent drops.

"It's beautiful."

"The simplest things in life are."

"You are so right. But I'm not simple."

He smiles, "You're simple enough … for me."

Her heart warms; she is reminded to stop analyzing their relationship and to quiet her expectations. She knows they will not always be by each other's side but sometimes she pretends they will. She plays house with him: cooks for him, eats his food, pours his beer, prepares his incense to burn, and washes the damp towels after the bath. She even brings him groceries sometimes. He quietly protests all of it but always makes her feel welcome. There is little room for her in his world, but he gives what he can. His daughters do not know about her; his ex-wife does.

He takes out his camera and shoots a picture of the single flower. His huge hands turn the lens to focus. She watches silently.

"Alright." And they begin walking again.

After some time, he stops her and shows her a green mountain leaf growing on the side of the path. He explains this leaf is the one used to wrap the sweet warm bean paste used in tea ceremony and Shinto food offerings to the Shinto gods. He gathers some to give to the priest at his local shrine. He takes out the special paper towel and plastic zip-lock bag he prepared for this very purpose. With a few quick gestures, he folds two wet leaves into a boat with mast and hands it to her.

"For when you decide to leave me."

She smiles a grimace and looks down. When she looks up again, his right hand cradles her chin and he kisses her. She melts in the chorus of raindrops falling around them.

They carry on for a time until she stops suddenly in her tracks. Rain droplets before them outline a perfect web in front of

73

her eyes. The spider must be in hiding or have vacated for a safer home. She reaches her stick up and pushes the web aside. It seems a shame to her to destroy such a perfect home, but there is no other way to pass. The earth falls away from them on either side. To the right they can see the valley of green trees below. To the left, the wet, green leaves disappear into darkness. She scrapes the web from the stick on the ground below and continues. She remembers the unexpected morning she went walking with her home-stay mother. They somehow ended up walking through the cemetery on the other side of the train track near their house. It had rained the night before and raindrops painted otherwise invisible spider webs between gravestones. Some of the spiders were hanging onto their homes; refusing that their hard work be destroyed by the weight of the morning rain. She took a picture of a single fuchsia-colored flower that grew next to the weathered wooden fence that encircled a section of grave sites. Later she painted a copy of the photograph into her journal, a perfect replica of the morning scene save the dew dropped webs. Her unskilled hand could never recount the silken perfection.

The rain picks up and the ceiling of trees no longer protects them. As soon as they come across a mountain cabin, they step inside. Others have gathered there. They smoke a cigarette Akira has kept dry. The coffee is still hot inside of the thermos. The others seem to intrude on their intimate world inside the cabin. As soon as the rain slows, they go outside and continue up the hill. The tops of these mountains are covered in trees. The peak is not obvious and they only stop when they realize their path has started to descend the other side.

They eat a simple lunch of rice and cold fish. More coffee, another cigarette, and they carry on down another path to the bottom. Her feet are cold and he rubs them over her wool socks on the train. She feels the coldness of her wet pants on her leg as she lifts her foot to him. A chill runs through her body and he promises her a warm bath.

THE PRACTICE

CHAPTER FOURTEEN
SHAKKEI TEMPLE, CHIBA, JAPAN

JANUARY, 2013

RIGHT THOUGHT

Shakkei is an interesting name for the temple where I am staying. I remember first being introduced to this word in graduate school at Columbia. My best friend was studying art history and specializing in East Asia. We took some classes together cross-listed between our two departments. In the aesthetic of a Japanese garden the word Shakkei is defined as "borrowed scenery." Some of our joint studies included Japanese art, theater and the art of Japanese Gardens. This borrowed scenery refers to elements that are not part of a Japanese garden but can be seen from the garden. In other words, it is the landscape surrounding the garden, the backdrop for the garden that can be viewed from different angles within a garden – a mountain, an adjoining forest, a group of city buildings through the trees.

I have come to understand that this temple is a borrowed scenery for me, a backdrop for the journey of my soul. While I identify with the temple – it is the space where I exist at this time – it is not a part of me. The body of this life is separate from the temple walls that surround me now. This temple is a vehicle for me to face the difficult questions that seem to define my life at the moment.

Shakkei Temple derives some of its revenue from a well-known garden which tourists come to visit. There is a separate entrance for visitors just around the corner from the main temple entrance. For a donation, "fortunes" can be obtained just inside of the entrance. This practice originates in the Chinese *I Ching*, or Book of Changes. A large urn holds one hundred and eight different wooden dowels that have been sanded and stained. At the flattened end of each wooden stick is an engraved, painted number. Donation amounts vary depending on how high the stakes are for a visitor. If a student is about to sit for entrance exams to university, for example, she might place a 1,000 yen bill in the donation box. If a regular visitor is making a pilgrimage to the temple, he might place 100 yen inside. After putting the coins into the box, the visitor reaches into the vessel to choose a dowel, which is immediately placed back inside again. He then walks to a tall wooden medicine cabinet of sorts, opens the drawer with the corresponding number, and reaches inside to take one paper fortune. All of the fortunes in any one drawer are the same. The first symbol on the paper indicates whether the fortune is "good," "bad," or "auspicious." Unlike those found in Chinese fortune cookies in America, many of these fortunes are not positive. There is a low tree to the left of a small Shinto temple where visitors tie their fortune after placing additional coins at the entrance of the shrine. The price to pay should be higher to counter a bad fortune received. Coins, however, are also paid in thanksgiving for a good fortune.

Japan is a society of duality and complexity. In the United States, it would be very odd to find a Jewish Star of David, for example, at a Catholic Cathedral. In Japan, Shinto and Buddhism exist in a symbiotic relationship. An elder friend of mine once said, Japanese are born Shinto and die Buddhist. Shinto is a religion of nature, recognizing *kami* or god spirits throughout the natural world. A *kami* might exist in a rock or a tree or a mountain. Shinto temples are often the site for festivals celebrating harvest, planting, and other life rituals. Buddhism, in societal terms, is understood as the vehicle through which Japanese revere ancestors. Buddhist temples are often the site for Japanese funerals. On average, as Japanese age, their attention shifts from Shinto practices to Buddhist pilgrimages. Many traditional Japanese homes have both Shinto offeratory tables where household received gifts are placed for a short period of time, and Buddhist mini-alters where pictures of ancestors are displayed. No tension exists between this co-existence. In other words, common people are not considered "Buddhist," or "Shinto;" there is no conflict between the duality.

During the first week of my stay, on one of my return trips from town, I walk through the garden gate. I recognize the man at the entrance counter. He smiles, bows and waves me through. Feeling somewhat self-conscious, I approach the donation box. I remove the 10,000 yen bill I have prepared folded in my pocket and place it in the wooden slot. Bowing my head, I silently pray for guidance and peace in my heart. The sticks are cold in my fingers. I stir them around like cake batter and finally fumble upon two. Struggling with which one to select, as I feel like the choice holds so much meaning. Inclined to start over, I ponder for a moment on this idea that I hold that there is only one right path for me to follow. Perhaps the stick I will choose will determine everything. Hesitancy paralyzes me until I realize that someone else has arrived behind me and is waiting. Clenching my fist slightly allows one to drop, and I remove the dowel. Number six. *Roku* in Japanese. With a deep breath, I place the stick back inside and approach the drawer set. I think to myself that a low number cannot be all bad. At first I do not find the drawer and then I realize that they are arranged top to bottom, right to left. Removing the long strip of paper, I see that the entire fortune is written in traditional Japanese. I recognize the character for "auspicious" on the top of the paper. Suddenly I feel silly to have played this little game with myself and danced with fate. I look around, sort of hoping that someone will see my helplessness and offer to translate. I walk back to the entrance to find someone to assist me. The man at the front gate recognizes me from our meal time likely, and explains to me that the traditional Buddhist language is very difficult. Assuring him that he can attempt to explain to me in Japanese, we agree to talk before lights out tonight. He will come to my room.

Placing the fortune in my pocket, I thank him and head back towards the garden. Shakkei. As I enter the garden, I look towards the edges to find what part of the landscape has been "borrowed." My mind continues to wander, seeking meaning, and I find myself thinking about the metaphors of life.

I walk through the garden of my life. Winding throughout the garden is a pebble path whose rocks are plentiful in places and sparse in others. The course of my own journey has been both deliberate and uncertain at different times in my life. The path has been seemingly random, as the path appears in this garden. Understanding, however, that the course of the path is well thought out, planned and sculpted, I intuit that the journey of my life holds some higher meaning with an energy that is greater than simply what I can observe.

As I walk through the garden, my eyes are drawn to a part of the landscape that the path does not take me towards just yet. I have to carry on, continue on the journey, and wait for its course to take me in the direction it will. Sometimes the wait has been long, like finding an enduring love; sometimes I merely turn a bend around a single tree and I arrive at an unforeseen place.

In the foreground, lush green moss has spread seemingly out of control and now blankets a larger space. For me, it is like the warmth of a lover, the uncontrolled passion and love that a new couple experiences. The gardener has allowed it to spread beyond its planned borders. My own life's experiences in new love were like this. Love took over pieces of me, and places in my heart that I did not expect to give. There were places in my soul filled with love for another that I wasn't even aware existed. Love is soft and cool, warm and dense, much like the moss that blankets this space. I think about this for a time. Does love fade? Can love die, shrink, or change? Or does love become muddled by other things in our world?

79

Perhaps love simply becomes unseen, unrecognized, unlived, even though it still exists in its deep experienced intensity.

The stone lantern is my faith. In walking through the garden, one might even miss sight of this subtle feature sitting quietly, tucked behind the base of a tree or hidden in the deep shadows of an overhanging branch at the back of the garden. When it is dark, the lantern is lit and readily seen; in the filtered sun of a bright day, it stands remotely waiting. The lantern is stone and strong, but its value is really only experienced in darkness.

The brown dried moss growing down the vein of a boulder hides the deep scar that runs through the orifice. The lines on our faces, the memories of hurt in our hearts, are both perfect and painful. Some scars represent beauty in our lives, like stretch marks from carrying a baby in one's belly. I have a single one just below my navel. I remember the excitement I felt when I discovered it; forever tattooed by the experience of carrying new life. Our lives would not be the same without being weathered, yet we fight these signs, the wrinkles – even the laugh lines – at their first appearance. Hiding the canvas of our lives doesn't seem to make sense.

The tall bamboo grove represents my friendships. Each trunk seems to grow so strong towards the sky. When the wind blows they bang into each other, echoing a hollowed-out symphony of percussion. New stalks grow in the shade of the others. Each stalk is beautiful on its own, but the greatest splendor is heard only in the context of a grove, like the resounding laughter, stories and tears that define the interactions and connections we have with our friends

80

The old wooden well, my family, stands as a constant, worn memorial to nourish, replenish, and restore. It is the reserve source of sustenance. It feeds so much of the garden, providing an absolutely necessary element, yet its value is hidden deep below the surface.

The small, red maples splash intermittent color on the subtle landscape of the garden, like paint on walls. These strong colorful trees represent my son in my mind. Regardless of the years that pass, the trees' vibrancy will always be the delicate pieces of the garden, expressing simple beauty. Their vibrant presence adds such beauty to the landscape. These trees are nurtured and cherished, drawing our attention and great affection.

The veins of water that course through the garden collect in a *koi* pond towards the middle of the garden. Life's passions blended with my inner self are the blood coursing through my own body – the substance that drives my life, washes me clean, and flows outward towards those I love.

There is a Japanese garden at the botanical museum on Vancouver Island. One day, Alan and I watched as our son ran through the sculpted landscape. We watched as he ran off ahead of us along the path, hand in hand with his favorite cousin, to explore the water trickling somewhere down the way. We hesitated for a moment to let them run wild, but the sweetness of their embrace left us speechless and unwilling to reel in their spirits.

They found treasures of the simplest kind: a fallen red leaf, a perfectly-round pebble, a bird sitting on a high branch. We remarked in awe of each, impressed that they found such pleasure in nature.

Once around the garden was not enough for them. Unlike most whom strolled slowly in one circular direction and exited, our scouts traversed the landscape defying all physics of linearity and termination. Finally we sat at the end of a bridge that capped the trickling stream below. They eventually found their way to us.

Later that night, sitting in our hotel room, I told Alan of the term *shakkei*. We both agreed that we would somehow consider our family life a success if we had become the borrowed scenery, the backdrop, for the gardens we hoped our son would create in his life. If we could be present enough to lend some of ourselves to the view of his world, yet at a distance enough to allow him to create a garden in his own right, well then we would have considered ourselves successful as his parents. As the children ran back to our arms at the bridge in the garden, cheeks red from running in the fresh air, we felt joy in our hearts to know we had allowed them to explore the garden on their own terms.

As I walk through the garden at Shakkei Temple, I do not feel how the garden has borrowed landscape from beyond its walls. The peripheral plants seem to have enclosed the space in a self-contained area. Many of the trees along the edge of the walls are overgrown, creating a lot of shade, and hiding from view that which lies beyond the walls. I feel safe here, perhaps because I cannot see what is outside of these walls. Even in the cold of winter, I long to stay here, sitting on this bench as long as the afternoon light will allow.

Thinking back again to that afternoon on Vancouver Island, I cannot trace in my mind how Alan and I got from appreciating the gifts of our life to such frivolity with the hearts of those whom we love. With a single choice, the beauty and intimacy of our lives was destroyed. How is it that two people fall in love, weather the storms of infant-induced sleepless nights, career changes and illnesses, and then seek abandonment and refuge in the arms of another? Seeking the answer to this riddle haunts my every thought of each day, and I feel lost. I feel somehow betrayed, not only by those who promised their love but also by the universe in which I once felt safe. Is Alan's life purpose predominantly a part of my garden, or am I an actor on his stage? Whose journey is the narrative? Whose story is the primary and whose life is the sub-narrative? Is there something each of us is meant to work through with the other? Has my life unfolded exactly the way it must in order for me to learn an important lesson that defines my existence? My therapist proposed a pattern of emotional abuse. I struggle to reconcile this concept with the moments of beauty we have shared. In so many ways the diagnosis of shared paths feels more comfortable. Perhaps I choose this explanation, because the pain of ending our marriage is too much to bear.

One thing I am beginning to understand is that I fabricate meaning around all sorts of events and relationships in order to explain the landscape of my life. Essentially, I decide why something has happened and what it means for my existence and journey. The "meaning" defines the discourse of my "story." I recognize that through interpretation I filter what has happened to me to those whom I love. I distill meaning, picking and choosing what elements of life I will recognize, give meaning to, and make "real." My first lesson with Nishida-sensei will be tomorrow. He has asked me to think about the stories that I create and live by. After my visit to the garden, I decide to make a list of stories and meaning tonight after my temple friend's visit to interpret my fortune. This seems like appropriate timing.

The temple bell rings in my ears and I am drawn away from my thoughts. My toes have frozen in my boots and burn as I hurry back to the compound. Even this pain is a sliver of grace, a safe refuge from my past and from the future. An excitement flutters in my belly to think of my anticipated evening visitor, dressed as a monastic student.

Chapter Fifteen

Shakkei Temple, Chiba, Japan
January, 2013

Right Thought

Today I received a letter from home. Just the sight of his writing, perfect letters on the flimsy airmail stationary I left on his bureau the night before I left, brings wetness to my eyes. I think for a minute of the bottom of his feet resting off the edge of his bed while he thinks of what to write. His sandy hair curls at the ends where it meets the nape of his neck. For a moment I allow myself to miss being with him. My sobs are not quiet. Is he alright? Does he have enough clean socks? Is he getting up on time for school? Does he know I love him? Is he lonely? Does he feel abandoned by me? Tears choke me and I struggle to catch my breath. What have I done? My shaking hands fumble with the envelope, afraid to rip even a single bit of the tissue-like paper. My tears drain dark spots onto the crepe paper, like unblotted ink. He begins.

Hi Mom!

Thanks for the paper. I
found it in my room
when I got home from
school. Everything here

is cool. I hope your trip is good. Dad and I are going skiing next weekend in Vermont. He said I can bring Dan if I want. His parents are thinking about it. He has some project due next week. Hopefully he can come.

Dad told me that you want him to move out for good. I really don't want you guys to get divorced. Can you please think about it again, Mom? That would really suck. John's parents got divorced last year and his mom moved to Boston. Why can't you guys just work it out? Dad even said he would think about it if you would. Think about it, Mom. Please...

I miss you.
Love,

Will

The tremble is uncontrollable. Fear spirals into a downward funnel. I am sucked into a black hole, a place where I cannot find my breath. I lie back on the *tatami* floor and close my eyes. My head is spinning with obsessive thoughts. My belly burns with nausea. Here I sit at a desolate temple somewhere in Japan held captive by my fear, while my son skis with his dad; I will lose them both.

I hear a gentle knock at my door. My fingers wipe away the wetness draining onto my cheeks. My fortune teller has arrived. I had forgotten. Calling for him to please wait one moment, I fumble to find tissues in my backpack. I blow my nose, look at the mirror in my compact, and accept the fact I will not be able to hide the tears. Still, somehow, I feel safe here.

Sitting on my heels, I slide the *shoji* door open easily and bow. Kimoto-san bows as he enters and sits just inside the door on his heels.

"So, let's see about this fortune." I notice he has brought several dictionaries, an old dictionary of ancient characters, a modern Japanese dictionary and a well-worn Japanese-English version.

"Oh, it's just here." As I hand him the narrow strip, I notice my hands are trembling. He does also, pausing, he looks up at me and our eyes meet for just a moment. He does not ask if I am alright, but he sits quietly for a moment with me, as if offering me the gift of silence. I breathe for just a moment, drawing the gift in deeply through my nostrils. I pray for my thoughts and fears to quiet.

"Okay. There are three sections. The first is your work or life practice. The next is your family.

And the last is your personal … uh, how do you say, your love life?"

"Ah, my personal life. Yes." I nod but my eyes fall to the floor in front of him.

"In your work or practice, the paper says there will be movement. You could change your home, for example, or travel, or change your job. These are the types of things it lists."

"Does it say if it's a good change or a bad one?"

"Here it says it is uncertain. Something like proceed with caution."

"OK."

"The next section is for your family. It also says something like change."

"Change? Does it say something more specific than that?"

He hesitates for a moment. His gaze holds at my eyes for a few moments. He looks serious and his eyes are almost wet.

"It says, death, actually."

I feel a lump in my throat. My heart seems to cease in its cavity and my mind stands empty.

"But you need to understand it says here this can mean the end of a relationship, change or movement, divorce, *or* death."

"Wow, all good things … which to choose." I say sarcastically in English. He doesn't understand my slight attempt at humor. He looks at me confused. I realize I have put him in a very difficult position.

"I'm sorry. I understand." For a moment, my eyes must show deep longing, for another time, another place. "It is just that I, I mean my family has been through a difficult time. I'm sorry."

"I understand." He looks back down. "There is one more thing."

"Yes?"

"Your ... personal life?"

"Yes."

"Connection. No, it says to connect again. How do you say that?"

"Reconnection? Reunion?"

"Ah, yes, reconnection. There is a reconnection to the past, a past life, an old friend, an old love, something like that."

Confused, I thank him for coming. He seems distracted, and gathers his books. As he turns on his knees to start towards the door, I reach out and touch his arm. I know it's a very "American" thing to do, but I look into his eyes and pause a moment.

"Kimoto-san, thank you. This is really helpful, and I'm grateful for your wisdom."

"Engle-san," he starts, "you have all of your answers in your heart. You don't need to read fortunes."

I smile, knowing he is right.

"All that you seek is already right here."

"*So, desu ne,*" I agree.

CHAPTER SIXTEEN

SHAKKEI TEMPLE, CHIBA, JAPAN
JANUARY, 2013

Nishida-sensei has asked me for another "story." I feel embarrassed that I seem to always write about men who have been in my life. I try to make a joke with him about it. He doesn't laugh, but instead tells me that some people have similar themes continue to show up in their lives until they learn the lessons they need to learn. He encourages me not to filter or think about him as an audience, explaining that the purpose of my work is for my own peace and well-being. This work and his presence are the vehicles through which I explore my own journey.

Sado Island, Niigata, Japan
Late May, 1994

She takes a bus to Niigata City, and transfers at the train station. The connection is quick but she boards in plenty of time to catch the local train to the north side of the city. The harbor is there waiting for her: alive and noisy. Even on this Friday afternoon, vendors are set up along the dock selling dried squid jerky and fried octopus balls with sweet sauce. She has a few minutes before she must board her ferry.

"Excuse me. Can I rent a bicycle on Sado Island?" She stops to ask at the tourist information booth.

"Yes, but they are a bit more expensive there."

"Thank you."

She heads over to look at the make-shift tents covered in slimy squid. The squid is purchased directly from the boats that come in to sell their goods. It is carried up in large buckets, rinsed once again and hung to dry on the straw covered bamboo racks.

"It is fresh – just caught this morning."

"How about these?" She points to the already dried squid on an adjoining rack.

"Oh, yes, these are ready to eat."

"They look delicious. I'll take some."

The wrinkled man hands her a cellophane bag filled with chopped up pieces of the dried flesh. It is stapled shut at the top and has a large sticker imprinted with the shop's name.

"Thank you."

He hands her an extra bag of squid spiced with wasabi.

"Present for you," he says in English. He bows slightly, laughing and looking away, embarrassed to have spoken the little English he knows.

"Thank you very much."

She walks away towards the boat but stops at a vending machine to buy some hot tea in a can. She chooses one oolong tea and one sweet milk tea for dessert. They are each so hot they burn her hand. She puts them into the plastic bag along with her squid, and boards the ferry.

The boat has a large enclosed sitting area to protect its passengers from the cold, harsh weather of

91

the strait. The winds here blow down from Siberia across the Korean peninsula and towards Japan. They hit Sado Island first. The air is cold throughout the entire year. Today is the first day of April. The sun is shining through the blue sky but the wind is freezing. She climbs the stairs to the top of the boat and sits in the covered area. She opens her squid and has a few bites, washing it down with the warm oolong tea. The combination of flavors is perfection.

There is a quiet excitement about her. She is heading out on her own to a Tibetan Buddhist weekend retreat on Sado Island. The leader of the group is an American guy in his late twenties. He spent nearly six years with the spiritual descendent of the Dalai Lama in Tibet. When the Dalai Lama was exiled in 1959, the Chinese government refused to allow another to take his place. A spiritual successor was eventually chosen and authorized by the Chinese government in 1989; he was only 6 years old and hardly a threat at that time. Our retreat leader lived in Tibet and studied with him and his instructors for years. He now tours Asia, his mission both spiritual and political. His retreats always include information regarding the grave political situation of the Tibetan people. He collects donations for his retreats, subtracts meek personal expenses and sends the remaining funds to support the Tibetan spiritual plight. Additionally, he guides attendees through specific meditations focused on purity, compassion, and knowledge.

Her trip to the island today is somewhat spontaneous; she only met the retreat leader five days ago. When he invited her to come along, she could not refuse. Her interest is definitely spiritual but she cannot resist his charm and child-like passion.

The boat whistle blows. She finishes the last of her oolong tea and heads outside to watch the shore as their ship pulls away. Most of the people on board are heading to Sado for cherry blossom viewing and hot spring resorts. The air burns her face as she heads out the door to the front of the ship. She tucks her plastic bag with the remaining tea into her small backpack, slings it along her shoulder, and holds onto the white railing. Niigata looks like such a small city behind her now. Sado Island quickly comes into view on the clear day. She breathes in cool air; it burns her nostrils. A chill shudders through her body; the wind has caused tears to stream down her cheeks.

After five minutes she heads back inside and finds a seat facing forward. Her dark tea is still warm and she holds it in her palms between sips. She feels alive. She did not invite a friend to join her, and she is happy to be away from her regular world for a few days. The retreat begins tonight and will last until Sunday afternoon.

After 45 minutes, the boat nears the shore, she goes back outside again, and is surprised to find the air warm. The boat's engine slows and calm air settles in around her. She squints into the western sunshine. Seagulls swarm around the boat, looking for fish entrails or the occasional crumb of bread. The whistle sounds in her ear just before they dock. She is one of the first to disembark. Walking confidently towards the stores she sees vendors selling the same goods on this side of the strait. She laughs to recognize the name on the banner above the squid vendor as the same that is on the cellophane package in her hand. She bows to the woman sitting under the banner, as though she knows her. The woman bows back.

Her rough map tells her to head south out of town. Within minutes she is outside of the small village. Rice patties surround her. The fields are newly planted and mostly mud. Small green sprouts stand perfectly placed in long rows, not a single stalk is out of place. The fields are empty now as it is late afternoon. A lone man walks towards his home along the dirt embankment separating the fields. Peddling, she passes several older women bent over their bicycles returning home from the markets. Their baskets are filled with fresh vegetables, fruit and fish. After busy mornings working in the fields, they head to the market to buy goods to top off their evening menus and to socialize with friends. Their dark eyes look up at her from under their straw, cone shaped hats. A few of them almost lose their balance as they ride towards her and falter, surprised to see a single, foreign woman peddling along through their neighborhood. She quickly realizes she is on the wrong side of the road. She moves to the left and this makes her passing, and theirs, much easier.

Her legs burn as the chain on her bike seems to stick from lack of oil. She has been peddling for just over an hour and estimates that she is nearly halfway there. A few kilometers back she made a wrong turn. A kind woman on a bicycle righted her before she had gone too far. The sky is starting to darken. Even though her legs are tired, she tries to pick up the pace, cursing the late morning slumber that caused her to miss the early bus to the city. The wind is cold again blowing against her cheeks. She realizes that she must have rounded the southern part of the island because the wind is now blowing directly into her face making the bike ride all the more challenging.

The burnt sky turns to black save the dark blue horizon to her left. She is heading north now along the western shore. Sado Island is only six kilometers narrow at its widest point. In the dark she misses her final turn. She enters a town that is not on her hand-drawn, photocopied map and she realizes she must turn around. The second time, she does not miss the dirt road to the right which narrows towards the ocean.

The road is very bumpy and difficult to maneuver in the dark. Deciding to save herself a potentially embarrassing entry, she dismounts her bike and walks along pushing it from the side. A sigh of relief and exhaustion leaves her as she parks in front of a wooden house. Hearing the sound of English through lit windows, she knows that she is finally in the right place.

Everyone's eyes turn towards her as she enters the room and she is suddenly embarrassed to have travelled so far, without really knowing anyone here. She feels very alone, an outsider, and wonders why she worked so hard to be here. The group has just finished eating. A place is quickly arranged for her on the floor in front of a low wooden table. She sits directly on the tatami, as a woman brings her some bread and a bowl of thick bean soup. She talks with the Canadian guy sitting next to her at the table, but finishes her food quickly. She spots a carafe of hot tea across the room. Excusing herself for a minute, she retrieves two cups, bringing one to him.

Her clothes wet with perspiration, she feels chilled. She takes a sweater out of her bag and puts it on. Just as she opens her mouth to continue her conversation with the Canadian, she suddenly spots him. He is across the room, sitting casually against the

95

wall, one leg bent with his foot flat on the floor. Three women are talking with him; one is a middle aged foreigner, one is a Japanese woman in her mid-thirties and the other is a young foreigner. Before she finishes her tea, his eyes wander to her spot. He rises quickly and walks across the room to her without hesitation. She is in awe of his confidence.

"Hey, you made it."

"Yeah." A smile coats her face. There is not much more to say, but she realizes she must say something.

"Just after sundown. I almost killed myself on the dirt road leading in here."

"We put those pot holes there in hopes of producing some enlightenment."

"Well then there's no hope for me. I think I hit every one of them. I really gave it my best effort."

"It's good you made it." He looks right into her eyes. He holds her gaze for a long time; enough time to make her self-conscious. He is not. She smiles directly back for a few seconds but then lets her eyes shift to the floor.

"Yeah." Is that all she really has to say, after travelling more than 100 kilometers just to see him again, "yeah." She feels small and wishes she had not come.

"We're going to start again in a few minutes." He begins to stand. "Grab a spot up front."

"OK. Thanks."

He is overwhelmingly confident. While she knows that his charm is not what the weekend should be about, she can't resist. Did she really come here just to get to know him? He probably has a woman in every port. She could become a part of his entourage and travel all over the world on his coat tails. He probably has some "free love" thing going on with a whole bunch of people. Those "Buddha types" always do. For just a moment, she imagines being able to bear that. Some part of her thinks that type of situation demonstrates utter detachment and inner strength. She knows women like that; they seem aloof and strong and detached. In her head she tries to sort out whether this is the case or if they are seeking "sharing" relationships so they never really have to go deep and attach to another; if they succeed, they never really get hurt.

Suddenly he is sitting in the front of the room. He utters not a single word but starts to meditate, closing his eyes and breathing deeply. She throws her stuff to the corner of the room and heads over towards the front. She chooses a spot off to the side.

After a few minutes, he begins to speak. She raises her gaze for a minute to notice a young woman organizing some pillows and books around his area. She is pretty, long blonde hair, thin, comfortable in her own skin. She finds a place to the right and joins him in meditation.

The meditation is focused on purification. He walks them through the ritual.

"Imagine you are sitting half lotus, high upon a pile of cushions. Your right foot is hanging down, dangling in the air. Take a deep breathe in and exhale thoroughly. Continue, continue. Push the air out of your lungs until you feel you can no longer exhale. Continue to push the air out, further, further. Hold your chest empty and tight for just a moment..."

Around the room she can hear people breathing in before they are told, against their intentions. She listens, under his spell. Deeply, she wants to feel what he feels.

"…Breathe in through your nose, feel the warm white liquid fill your lungs and then pass into your blood stream. Your veins, your every muscle, your lymph nodes and nervous system fill with this white liquid. As the liquid fills your body and is pushed into every crevice, feel the top of your head overflow, pushing out all of the impurities."

He interrupts to explain to the group that sometimes this meditation causes women to begin to menstruate. Others might find a single drop of blood at the top of their heads where the power of deep meditation causes blood to be pushed to the surface of the skin and appear on the scalp. Then he continues.

"Feel every pore in your skin open up. You might notice that you are perspiring. With each subsequent inhalation, your body takes in more of the clean white liquid, and with every exhalation you should feel impurities leave your body."

They continue in quiet meditation for nearly forty-five minutes. She is tired, but at the end of the meditation, a lightness surrounds the room. Some begin talking. She sits quietly in full lotus. The girl who seems to be his assistant explains that she will shut off the lights. If anyone wants to bathe they may – down the hall. People should feel free to talk quietly but at this point he is going to sleep and if anyone else would like to do so they may.

She gathers her things to her corner of the tatami. Finding her toothbrush and a change of clothes, she heads down the hall for the bathroom. She feels slightly awkward not knowing anyone, but cannot pass up the opportunity to soak in the hot steaming water that she knows is filled with the strong minerals of Sado Island's sulfur stock. She is surprised to find the small shower area has a door leading outside. After washing, she walks towards the steamy glass door and pushes gently on the metal handle. It opens. Outside she finds a round stone-lined hot spring pool. Steam is rising off of the liquid. With only a hand-sized towel to cover the front of her body she walks towards the steam. There is one person already inside but the steam is thick. She enters silently. Wringing the water out of her towel, she folds it and places it on her head. She sits for a long time until she hears the person across the way get out. She realizes it was a man as he walks towards an opposite door to reenter the building. She is surprised by her lack of embarrassment. Somehow this entire experience seems asexual. That is, except for him.

She wakes to the sound of feet shifting on tatami. A window is open and a cold wind is coming in. Her eyes open in the darkness. She snuggles into the blanket she brought with her. She is warm and her cheeks are cold. For a moment, she is sitting in the back seat of her mom's station wagon. It is early summer and the windows are down. They are returning home from a long weekend at her grandmother and grandfather's house on the Cape. Her brother is lying in the "way back" sleeping. Her mother is driving on the freeway in silence. She cannot hear the radio because of the wind in her ears. She closes her eyes again. The wind makes them tear and sting but she insists that the window be open. She loves the feel of the cold wind; she snuggles into the plaid, wool, stadium blanket. It is scratchy but somehow she would have it no other way.

She sits up in half lotus, breaths in the chill on her skin. The air is fresh and cold in her lungs. The salt on her hair makes it soft. After twenty minutes or so the sky turns a grey blue and she gets up to go to the kitchen. She finds the large rice maker on the counter. She takes rice from the closet, washes it several times in the large metal sink. It rinses clear and she adds fresh water. Within ten minutes the rice is steaming and the air is filled with the taste of breakfast. She finds vegetables and pickles in the refrigerator. She cooks the greens in water and garlic. She slices the hard pickles and arranges them on two long plates.

"Good morning." She is startled by a husky morning voice.

"Good morning."

"Coffee?"

"No. There isn't any."

"No, I'm offering."

"Really?"

"Yes." He says a bit grouchily.

"Yes, please."

He begins to slowly find his way around the kitchen. A cupboard door slams shut by accident. He is asleep enough not to be bothered by the sound. She removes the plastic dishes from the cupboards where they were placed clean the night before. Quietly, she carries them through to the great room where most lie still sleeping. She notices that his futon at the front of the room is empty; a blanket toppled over his sleeping place. She sees his t-shirt thrown to the side and wonders if he is in the bath.

It takes several trips before enough dishes are on the table. She begins arranging the plates, guessing how many people will eat. She returns to the kitchen to retrieve the forgotten chopsticks. Coffee is ready.

"Thank you." She swallows deeply.

"Ahh, this is so good. I'm Elise, by the way."

"Richard."

"Nice to meet you, Mr. Richard.

He smiles. "Thanks for making all of us breakfast."

"My pleasure. The rice is almost done and veggies are hot if you're interested."

"Not yet." He says.

"Let me know when you're ready."

"Soon."

"Okay." She smiles at him and thinks to herself that he is kind of cute ... tossled hair, blue eyes, great smile.

She opens the door, chopsticks in hand, just as the two of them come in from the outside, their bodies wet, water dripping from their hair. She stops for a minute, surprised to see them. She considers lurching back into the kitchen, but decides to continue her task. Her heart is pounding in disappointment. They are whispering quietly to each other, smiling, laughing. She pretends not to notice them. He puts his dry t-shirt from the floor over his wet body. She places the last pair of chopsticks and goes back into the kitchen. The cooking light has changed from "cook" to "warm" on the rice cooker. In a minute the door pushes open and his barefoot body enters. She can see the wet through his t-shirt, clinging to his chest underneath. Her legs feel weak.

"Good morning." His smile radiates.

101

"Good morning." She cannot help but return the smile. His childlike enthusiasm is enough to alter anyone's state.

"Ahh." He walks to her and hugs her. "Breakfast. Thank you."

She blushes a deep red from his sudden attention.

"Can I get you some?"

"In a minute. I am still absorbing my morning swim."

"What? You went in the water?" She asks trying to pretend she hadn't noticed.

"Oh, yeah." He sings.

"It is freezing."

"Did you go in?" His question is suddenly serious.

"No. Are you crazy?" She second guesses her harsh response. She fears impressing on him that she would not do something like that. With him, she might do anything. This is the problem.

"The wind blows in from Siberia. Were you a polar bear in another life?"

"I thought I was in this life. I don't look warm and cuddly?" He teases her.

"Polar bears are not warm and cuddly. They are highly territorial."

"Yes, this I am not." They are silent for a moment.

Richard comes back into the room. The sudden activity in the kitchen disrupts the moment.

"Shall we?" he suddenly says.

She unplugs the rice maker, and follows him into the other room. She returns to the kitchen for the warm vegetables. The miso soup from the night before is reheating on the stovetop. Richard offers to carry the pot of boiling soup into the main room. He burns his finger on the metal handle before she hands him a kitchen towel. She follows him in with the ladle.

Everyone sits to eat, Richard taking the spot next to her. They eat quickly, talking occasionally. She feels present and happy.

Soon, they are sitting again to meditate. After nearly an hour of prostrations, their leader suggests that everyone go outside and find a place to meditate alone. She steps outside for the first time of the day. The wind is blowing strongly and she tastes the salt in the air. The path curves off to the right and then sharply down towards the water. At the path's elbow, she finds a sole tree.

The base of the tree is nestled with low brush to shield the wind. She huddles into a spot there, sitting on top of her sweater. She opts to wrap her meditation blanket instead around her shoulders. Sitting with her eyes closed she listens to the strong sound of the waves breaking against the rocks below. The sound is muffled by the wind gusting against her ear drums. The sky is overcast, gray, and bruised in the distance. Rather than meditating immediately she sits for some time thinking of home and missing her family. An ironic salt air blows hard enough to dry her tears before they fall, leaving only crusts of salt below each eye.

The wind changes suddenly to blow from behind her and then quiets. The tree to her back shields her and she feels warm. A daydream of sorts consumes her meditation.

A fog is rising through the jungle, as night is well under way. She has been hiking for nearly twelve hours. She is suddenly alone. Her teammates have disappeared into the fog. The sounds of their voices echo in the distance. A sole monkey harps loudly from above, cursing his mate below. She is alone. Max had promised to meet her, hours before, at the last checkpoint.

The fog is thick now and the forest is dark. A sudden fear causes her to rise. She knows the path leads steeply up the hill, but she cannot find her footing. The stone steps have been carefully laid equidistant from each other. Two breathes in, one long breath out; she trusts her feet to methodically climb the incline. The fear in her belly fuels her endurance. She steps slowly and is long to tire. The path clears to a recent road built to allow military trucks to climb the mountain to access radar surveillance. The gradual incline of the road is a welcome change but soon becomes more tedious than the even stone steps from the path. The road dumps her onto a field of grass, where a full yellow moon clears the distant slope. Just to the right of the peak, the perfect sphere appears larger than the top half of the mountain before her. She leaves her fears in the darkness behind her. Walking faster now she hopes to make up the time she sat waiting for Max below. Only for a few seconds she thinks of the others she left behind. Their distant voices muted by the trees, she imagines him scrambling to find her in the darkness. Vengeance longs for him to feel panic and fear at her absence. He will sit shaking, helpless in his sweat soaked business suit, briefcase slung onto the ground at the base of the rock on which he sits. His delay is his loss. She is riding the wind above. Fear causes her to feel guilty remorse. His busy schedule and impending trip to Shanghai caused him to lose track of the time. A final phone call on this Friday afternoon ran too long. He missed the bus that runs on the hour by a full ten minutes. It took him fifteen minutes of running back and forth across the street to hail a taxi. HK$320 later he is running to her checkpoint. He misses her by a minute. They have always missed each other by a narrow

104

margin; she tests his love and collects evidence of its failure to prove the voices in her head wrong.

She runs past a group of soldiers, chained together at the ankles, marching in line with an armed man in tow. She looks back at them; they do not even notice her. The night is clear but their averted eyes remain so. She looks back again. Their eyes are black holes, no white, no distinctive pupils; just black. She runs faster. The next time she turns around they are gone.

The sweat on her brow is dripping into her eyes causing them to sting. Panic shoots up her spine. Her quads burn. Her hamstrings are tight. She chases the fear in her belly. She is lost; she is alone. The moon has shrunk back behind the mountaintop which seems to be further and further away. Laughter forces her to look left but only an empty field is reflected in her eyes. She drops her pack. A pain in her right ankle makes her run slow to a limp. Sitting on the side of the road, she massages a cramp out of her calf. Her heart races her breath and wins. She manages a few deep inhales and forces saliva down her parched throat. Someone grabs her shoulder; she loses consciousness.

She wakes startled. His face frightens her; his hands are on either shoulder.

"What? What?" She is panting to catch her breath; the wind blows again into her nose.

"It's okay. You're alright." His voice is still, calm, reassuring.

"Oh, my G-d." She is laughing shamefully, looking away embarrassed.

"I didn't mean to scare you."

"It wasn't you. I was dreaming, I guess."

"Are you alright?"

"Yeah. I guess. I mean, I don't really understand. What was I dreaming about?" She holds her forehead in her hand and tries to remember.

105

"I was hiking with friends and then I was alone. I was really afraid. I was on top of this mountain. There were soldiers. I was running and then sitting and then someone grabbed me."

He looks in her eyes and listens quietly. When she stops for a moment, he asks, "What did you feel?"

"Afraid, abandoned, alone…"

"Is that what you're afraid of, being alone?"

"Yes." She says embarrassed. Tears well up in her eyes. "I don't know if I'm afraid of love or of losing love. I think that I am so focused on losing the one that I love that I forget to love him."

He smiles a knowing smile. His eyes follow the horizon and look back at her.

The wind cannot dry her tears this time. They fall to the sea below. She is surrounded with salt. She feels utterly alone.

They sit silently for a while longer. It is as though each of them is sitting alone on top of this cliff overlooking the ocean. No words, no eye contact, no gesture, and no pretense – they are simply sitting beside one another. He gets up after some time, touches her shoulder gently, and heads back towards the building.

She sits with eyes closed for a few minutes longer, trying to recreate the scenes of her dream. She recalls feeling freedom as the yellow moon rose above the mountain. Where did that sense of liberty come from, as she walked along alone in the dark, the empty eyes of the soldiers staring back at her? Why didn't she run back to her base camp, her teammates, her boyfriend, safety? She realizes that she doesn't trust, not even those people closest to her.

Later when she returns to the group, she feels some release. A cup of tea warms the tingling in her

106

fingertips. Her head is filled with so many thoughts. Fear of abandonment and desire for isolation, it is the dichotomy of vulnerability and shame that closes her off. She never really dives into a relationship, and in isolating herself, she ultimately assures abandonment.

In the late afternoon, she descends the cliff that holds her both captive and safe from the stormy sea. Salty bubbles mark the water line along the sand. The air is calm but the waves are enormous, crashing near the shore. She removes her clothes and tries not to think about the impending drop off. What is it about deep water that scares people? Ten feet seems so much safer than fifty; you can drown the same in both. Sharks seek shallow water when they are hungry.

Empty mind, empty thoughts, empty, empty.

She splashes hard as she dives into the waves. Her skin burns from the cold. Immediately she tries to stand and cannot.

Don't think of your dangling legs. You are alone. The water is empty.

She begins to swim parallel to the shore. At first, she is out of practice, gasping for breath after two full strokes. The rhythm of the swelling sea surrounds her body. She changes to a breath every one and a half strokes. The water drips from her face.

She turns towards the shore and treads water. She considers exiting here and walking back along the shore.

She throws her right hand over her head and starts again. Her legs burn – tired, cold, both. A bit of water gets into her nose and she blows hard. She stops after a time and realizes the black heap of clothes on the beach is already behind her. The tide must have pushed her further along on the way back. She swims towards the shore. The breaking waves throw her, literally, onto the sand. She laughs out loud. The top of her head aches badly from the cold water and her fingers are white numb. Lying flat on the beach, naked, she shivers at the air colliding with her skin. Every pore closed desperately conserving body heat, every hair standing on guard, every nerve vibrating to produce warmth – she feels envigorated. She walks into the water again to wash off the sand. Her clothes feel sticky and limp from the salt air. Carrying her shoes in her left hand she heads up the rocks.

A shadow stands high on the cliff and turns away. By the time she has crested the cliff, the form is nowhere to be seen.

Later that night, somewhere between dusk and dawn, she feels a hand on her leg. She wakes to his face. He motions for her to follow. Turning back she grabs her blanket and sweater, heading outside behind him.

Lying on the beach on top of her blanket, he lights a cigarette. She inhales deeply and holds the smoke captive in her lungs.

"Coffee and now cigarettes?" she smiles at him.

"You don't seem very "Buddhist" half asking a question.

"It's all about the non-distinction, baby." They laugh together

They listen to the waves and count the stars. The night is remarkably clear considering the overcast day it follows. She wonders if their exhalations blew the clouds away. He pushes up onto one arm and looks at her. Slowly, she turns her head to his gaze. He leans down slowly, as though waiting for a refusal, and kisses her on the lips. She smiles immediately and he knows it was not a mistake.

"You taste salty."

"Mmmm," she agrees.

He smiles, seeming to look past her, and leans down again. This kiss is deep with passion.

"I was in the bath with you the other night."

"That was you?"

"Yep."

"How did you know it was me?"

He smiles.

"I know these things. I wouldn't have offered you coffee if I hadn't first seen you naked."

"Inspected the goods?" She teases him.

"I like kissing you."

"I like you kissing me."

She knows that tonight will be the first and last of their times together. She heard him mention to someone that he is leaving Japan the next Thursday to study in Montana.

"I know you're leaving."

"Would you believe me if I told you I can ride the time and space continuum?"

She smiles back at him.

"I wouldn't doubt that you could transcend some version of that."

"We might meet again. America's not such a big country. I'll be in Montana for the next four years. Come find me."

She smiles and turns away. This one will leave before she has the chance to push him away. Some intuitive place inside of her knows she isn't ready for him anyway. The fear of her meditative dream, like a guidepost, pulls her toward a future where she will have to confront her need for others to fill the hollow places inside of her. She pulls men close and wallows in the relief of not being alone. After the excitement of the beginning wanes, she begins to hear voices inside of herself that tell her she isn't good enough; he will leave her. Then she begins to collect evidence, and before long "he isn't the right one for her," and she leaves.

Just after chores, I walk the dark hall to Nishida-sensei's quarters. Carrying a notebook in hand, I feel butterflies in my stomach. I have written many lines about my stories and I am quite sure I am entirely uncomfortable talking about what the pages contain.

"Engle-san, please," he gestures towards the low desk basking in the late morning sun.

"Thank you."

"How are you finding your time here?"

"Honestly, full of a lot of thought, when I expected to find much silence."

"Ah, yes, those voices in our heads; they fill any possibility of empty spaces."

"That is very true!"

"Emptiness does not come without effort. Most of us have a lifetime of words, thoughts, and experiences that we must clear before we can feel the gift of nothingness."

"I have spent some time thinking about those experiences," I say placing my notebook on the table.

"Ah, yes. And how did you find that?"

"Difficult...   filled   with   regret... disappointing... pathetic."

"Ah, then I guess it was a worthwhile effort."

"Really?"

"Yes. What do you observe?"

I am silent for a long time, uncertain of what to reveal. I open up the notebook, turn the pages, and consider reading. Nishida-sensei places his hand in front of me and taps the table.

"Engle-san, it is not important what the pages say. They are simply the details of what has happened. What do you observe here," and he reaches out to point towards the center of my forehead with his middle finger. Taking a deep breath, I avert my eyes towards the center of the table meditatively.

"Regret... awareness... blame..." slowly the words flow from my throat deliberately and with new ease... "anger... sadness... death."

As Nishida-sensei takes a deep breath, his shoulders seem to fall, almost in relaxation or relief. I mimic his body language.

"Do you feel it?" He asks.

With a slight smile, I answer, "Yes." I raise my eyes and feel an uncontrollable smile paint itself across my face. I feel embarrassed to have such a reaction.

Finally he breaks the silence saving me from my feelings of self-consciousness. "When we acknowledge, like with meditation practice, when things come into our heads – thoughts, words, feelings, we are able to let go, or empty, our heads slowly. When you acknowledge your feelings, create a space for them, they will dissipate. They depart, and what remains is your present breath, only. This is ..."

"Freedom." The words fall from my mouth.

With a slight smile of satisfaction, Nishida-sensei says, "Yes. Exactly. What does this freedom mean to you?"

"Relief?"

"Yes, and as we finish today, I want you to consider 'nothingness.'" I am surprised that we will end so soon.

"Mmmm," I don't understand exactly but I feel that we have shared in something profound and I want to have time to consider what he has said. Nothingness. I feel a fleeting sense of understanding, and then I feel it leave me completely, and I am afraid that I didn't really get his point.

It is the end our meeting, and I ready myself to leave. Just as I begin to stand, Nishida-sensei begins to speak.

"The opposite of alone, is loneliness. In loneliness there is longing. Alone is just empty." Then, Nishida-sensei is silent. He gets up, returns to his desk, and begins working.

Feeling somewhat confused and embarrassed, I rise, leave the room and return down the long corridor. Lying on my tatami floor later, I am hit by a strong realization. Tears flood my eyes and 'I get it.'

In choosing to be alone, I create an emptiness, and in that space, I can create a life of complete fulfillment. When I stay in inauthentic relationships, I experience great loneliness. I cannot stop crying, but for the first time in a very long time, I feel safe; alone and safe in this world. Max, Richard, Akira, and Alan all feel very separate for the first time. I begin to understand my responsibility in how I experienced my relationships with each of them, but I am exhausted and I just want to sleep.

CHAPTER EIGHTEEN

SHAKKEI TEMPLE, CHIBA, JAPAN
JANUARY, 2013

RIGHT MINDFULNESS

For the past week, my afternoons have been spent studying calligraphy and tea ceremony. I enter the dank room and take my place behind a low desk. We sit *zazen* when we study calligraphy also; the practice is meditative and requires attention to the breath. The thick ink pours into the simple, stained, clay dish. A metallic smell fills my nose. I love the way the black liquid, having a mind of its own, finds its place on the paper before me. A random speck sometimes finds its own path when my brush first touches down. The ink soaks slightly into the paper along the edge of my stroke. For the first week here I wrote single characters each day. My sensei is now asking me to copy the text of the Lotus Sutra. A long scrolling paper on rollers is clamped to my desk. I write one character at a time. They dry quickly enough for me to roll them using the scrolling crank at the top of my desk. In the two hour practice I usually complete about one hundred and thirty characters. I have been criticized for writing too quickly. Knowing my time here is short, I feel an urgency to complete my work, the shoji, the Lotus Sutra, my "enlightenment."

The smell of incense burned long ago fills my nose. The excess ink drips down the side of the dish from my wet brush tip. The bristles curl slightly in one direction. Holding the brush perpendicular to the paper, I lower it towards the first stroke. My hands used to shake so badly in my youth. I could never stand before a class to give an oral presentation without hearing snickering laughter in my ears. I memorized all of my speeches the best I could to avoid having to hold a paper in my hands. I preferred talking to large groups of hundreds or thousands because I knew a podium would be provided to hide my shaking hands. Brain surgery was ruled out early, and removing splinters from my son's feet after a play date on Grandma's wooden deck was a near impossibility. My hand is steady now which surprises me. A simple breath is so powerful. Focusing on the air flow through my nostrils, onto the back of my throat and into my lungs, muscles tight in my abdomen, diaphragm strong – sometimes I think I can literally feel the clean oxygen in my blood, carrying nutrients and life through my body. Pushing impurities out of my pores, out of my lungs, from my liver, into my large intestines; I am pure and empty.

The muscles in my left arm have become so strong from this practice. Even more than the numbness in my legs from *zazen*, the soreness of my upper arm, shoulder and back was unbearable the first couple of days of practice. On more than one occasion droplets of sweat ruined a nearly perfect character I had drawn.

More than a week ago, my practice began with the character for heart-mind, emptiness and interconnectedness.

Kokoro – heart/mind/spirit – a simple character of only four strokes; very difficult to write well. Much like life -- the most simple, intuitive thing one can do is live, but to do it well is a challenge. It seems that to live haphazardly, with much spontaneity and disregard, is easy. But to live with mindfulness of oneself, of others, and of the chains that link our lives together is less simple. A simple exaggeration can be hurtful; a single comment about someone else can bring much sadness; an innocent decision can cause much harm to others. It is easy to live; it is difficult to live with compassion in mind, or rather with our mind in compassion. I have not achieved this but I am committed to practicing it.

Nashi or *sunyata* – emptiness – a difficult concept to grasp. If we are devoid of attachment, how can we love? If we empty our mind of thoughts, how can we be aware? If we expel noise and seek silence, how can we help others? This notion is difficult to negotiate. Specific attachment to the way we perceive something to be is what is at stake in Buddhist philosophy. Our biased attachment or expectation of the world, our relationships, and individuals causes much disappointment and suffering. If we allow ourselves to be open to the infinite possibilities of the universe – of who our loved ones might be or might become, of how our relationships might develop or end, of how much we affect the world we live in while also understanding much is beyond our control – we will find some inner peace and empathy.

In seeking to empty one's head of repetitive thoughts or negative perceptions, we open ourselves to a deeper awareness of our surroundings. It is a simple concept really: if a bucket is already filled with debris from cleaning the garden – weeds and bits of dirt – and the cover has been replaced for carrying to the compost pile, fresh rain that falls in the early morning cannot enter. Even if the bucket of my emotions is full, I seek to keep the cover off. Something will surely distill in the water that flows through the clutter of life that overwhelms my everyday thoughts. I have always said that your first thoughts of the day, the ones that come the moment you have just opened your eyes, are the clearest. The mind is cleansed each night as we sleep – thoughts and fears are emptied into our dreams. Perhaps these thoughts are the pure, distilled liquid that flows through this vessel of a body that I inhabit. I certainly have not found that I can empty my mind but I do experience how the gaps between my thoughts and anxieties have widened. These spaces are the place where I find clarity, acceptance, and forgiveness. This is the "emptiness" that my practice seeks.

Sorting through the clutter of thoughts and seeking silence, allows us to focus in on the most important aspects of our surroundings. In channeling our energies in this way we have the greatest opportunity to positively affect others. Being quiet in this world is a near impossibility. We fill silences with small talk; we quiet the tears of a child without listening to their real needs; we waste our time talking about others without caring for them at all. Emptiness is about seeking constructive silences that allow us to heal and nourish the world around us. It allows us to be presentl.

Aida – between/interconnectedness – the notion of an intimate relationship between our thoughts and actions and the rest of the world – spiritual, physical, metaphysical. We affect and are affected by people, their actions, their inaction, nature,

117

its destruction, its energy, animals, their needs, and their deaths. The mistake we make with this concept is to place ourselves at the center of interconnectedness. Humans often suppose we are at the center of our universe, at the apex of the pyramid. We are surprised by natural disaster as if we believe it was targeted at us and we are somehow undeserving of this destruction. We feel betrayed by our world. The chains of causation are not always clear, logical or explainable, but there is always a chain. The chain is not linear, but rather a matrix that ripples outward from an event, like concentric circles appearing on the surface of a lake after a single pebble has been thrown at its face.

Embracing our ineffable connection to our surroundings we take a huge leap of faith. We take absolute responsibility for our actions, which is daunting, and we give up the expectation that others should and can make us happy, which requires giving up an enormous amount of control over others. We begin to feel a deep sense of compassion for the world around us. We began to love, both as a means of understanding, and as a means of forgiveness, of ourselves and of others. We learn to live and to communicate on a higher level. There is nothing mysterious about this. It simply requires deliberate thought, deliberate action, and deliberate responsibility. When writing this character over and over again, I decide to explore the ways in which I have been responsible for creating the life I am living today. For a moment, I consider the possibility of forgiving myself, my family, and Alan.

The shadows of the trees have grown long in the garden outside of the window. Evening is arriving. A single bell rings outside. Caps are replaced; brushes are soaked for washing; paper is left to dry; the sound of footprints shuffling on the straw floor fills my ears. We enter the hall and separate to different corners of our temple home. I walk towards the well that stands outside in the back vegetable garden.

A homemade siphon fills my wooden bucket and I head towards the winter blooms I nurse in the makeshift greenhouse to check on their growth. Using a small wooden ladle, I give each plant a drink of fresh rainwater. The tomato leaves smell strong from sitting in the sun all day. Green, yellow and early orange-red balls hang heavy from the strong stalks. The peas are ready to be picked. The zucchini and eggplant are small. There will be a long wait until the eggplant has turned dark purple and grown long enough to pick. I empty my first bucket at the base of the persimmon tree. I will fill it three more times before all of the fruit trees are watered. The plums are ready for picking. I fill my empty bucket in minutes and take the sweet treasures to the kitchen. A few are set aside for offerings at the altar; many are washed for dinner; a few will be taken to our neighboring Shinto shrine in the morning. A simple cloth envelope will be folded around eight and set outside of their back gate before the sun rises. We keep their gods happy this way and remind our neighbors that we have them in our minds each day.

I return to the garden. After I fill my bucket once with dried weeds and dump them into the compost, I gather my tools. It is a strange thing, this respect of all living things. When I was a vegetarian who did not eat fish, poultry or meat, I questioned why I ate eggs and cheese. How could I justify these aspects of the food producing industry when I felt so

119

adamantly opposed to taking life? And we all laughed about the fruitarian joke in the film Notting Hill when the prospective suitor for Hugh Grant said that she only believed in eating fruits and vegetables that had already fallen to the ground, and had "died of natural causes." But, this version of "vegetarianism" is the only one that truly respects all aspects of life. Anyway, we remove weeds from our garden at the temple. We eat fruits, grains and vegetables. We are mindful of our sources of nutrition, but ultimately life energy is transferred as we consume plants and animals for our own existence. I pause for a moment to think of responsibility again. Perhaps if I go deep enough, if I get authentic with my thoughts, actions and feelings, I can quiet my noisy judgment of others and create some space to make something constructive in my life. If I stayed on my side of the sidewalk, I might get somewhere.

The silhouettes of the trees are like cut outs glued to the deep blue sky on the horizon. Forgotten stalks of rice hang over limbed teepees on the back side of the temple property frozen in the snowy air. I run my hand along the hard envelopes of grain as I walk by. For thousands of years, each grain of rice has gone through the same process on its journey to our tables. The more traditional Japanese believe it is sacrilegious to leave even a single grain of rice in the bottom of your bowl. Understanding that the same effort is extended to produce a single grain of rice or a thousand, they respect each morsel. To discard even a single grain of rice would be to waste an entire harvest. There is something in that, I think for a moment.

The hallway is now very dark. I wash my hands, arms, face and mouth very quickly. The long basin extends several meters in each direction, and it is empty. I have lingered too long in the garden, stroking rice. The others are surely already sitting for our evening meditation. I run quickly but quietly down the wooden corridor. Catching my breath, I step into the *zendo*; I am the last to arrive. Lowering my head, I walk briskly to my place. The minute I sit, the bell is struck and our breaths begin.

CHAPTER NINETEEN

SHAKKEI TEMPLE, CHIBA, JAPAN
JANUARY, 2013

RIGHT EFFORT

Being a foreigner in Japan is not easy. It has its good points and challenges. During the first year that I lived in the Japanese countryside my emotional state could be judged by how I reacted to the children's reactions to me. One day in the grocery store near my home, a young boy who was probably no more than three, peeked out from behind his mother's leg. Fumbling for money in my backpack, I didn't notice him at first. Suddenly I caught a glimpse of his big eye peering around at me.

"Konnichiwa." I greeted him with a slight bow, an attempt at humoring him.

"Gaijin! Gaijin!!!" He took off running past "the foreigner," around the corner and down the aisle. His mother bowed to me as she ran after him. His tears could be heard throughout the store. I felt the burn of everyone's eyes on me. I felt implicated for causing this poor boy to cry. My very presence was disturbing. Tears filled my eyes but I refused to let them fall. I longed for my own mother to wrap her arms around me, lovingly, in the same innocent way that little boy's mother calmed him. She was not here.

I longed to be invisible, to have my foreignness assimilated away. Yet, in this world, things like nationality partly define who we are. In the case of Japan, ethnicity is very important. But identity is a strange phenomenon. First of all, it is fluid. I tend to identify with whomever I am speaking. I begin to see myself like those who surround me, or I judge harshly those who are different than I in order to substantiate who I am. Perhaps everyone is the same, by nature, in this respect. I am not sure of the answer, but a lot of money and time have been spent on propaganda and political agendas to differentiate peoples and nations from one another.

I was born a Presbyterian; I lived my life as a Jew. Perhaps I will die Buddhist. Here, people say that they live Shinto and die Buddhist. There is something to be said about feeding the G-ds who surround you in life and honoring the ancestors who will welcome you beyond.

My Buddhism is about widening the gaps of silences in my life. In my practices of work and meditation, I seek a life of simplicity and quietude. In the gaps that I find, I am able to confront my feelings without attaching my actions to them. It is about accepting who I am, who I have always been. For me these weeks at Shakkei Temple have been about neutralizing the life that I have lived, and trying to make sense of it all. Having the forum within which to face my life, my relationships, their beginnings, and their ends, has been a rare experience. I do not feel void of attachment or even particularly enlightened, but I do feel that I can better understand some of the decisions I have made.

I understand now why I have hurt some very decent people, why I have forgiven some bad people, why I have sought love, acceptance, and acknowledgement, and the suffering I have allowed from all of these encounters. I respect people who can see others without judgment, although I have not often been able to do this personally. I surround myself with people who are comfortable to be by themselves.

All relationships have strings, but I have always sought those that were the longest. It is not that I shirk responsibility, it has just been that I understood from a young age that I need space in order to grow, change and live. The relationships that have failed in my life have done so because I was not able to loosen the strings that bound me to another person. Either I held them too tightly or they needed to hold me closer than I could be held at the time. These relationships have been a "longing-retreating" tug of war, where someone always ended up face down in a puddle of mud.

A sense of identity is only sustainable when the heartstrings that attach to us are loose enough to allow change. That is why labeling can be so painful: foreign, gay, Jewish, woman. By definition, life longs to be dynamic, ridden with growth and profound transformation, but unfortunate societal barriers exist to prevent this.

We are. I am. To come into someone's life and expect them to continue to be the person they were when you met seems like an odd expectation, yet so many people hold their loved ones to this supposition. We are surprised by change; we come to question and resent it. Suddenly in the midst of my life which has been characterized by fear of change, I am surprised by this fact.

What in my own life held constant? There are few things; change is one of them. It is often that we grasp understanding of something just when it becomes something else. This is the thing that has kept me alive to this day. In times when I have felt grave desperation, I have figured I may as well hang out for another day to see what happens. I can always end my life tomorrow. By the next day, it becomes apparent to me that the dualities of life exist always. Profound happiness cannot exist without great discontent, for it is often the by-product of deep discontent. The good times will cease as surely as the bad. "This too shall pass…" an inscription on the ring granted to a desperate king in a Ram Dass poem my brother sent me when I was in my early twenties living abroad. Equanimity is a remote trait in our fast paced world, but I still believe it is something worth striving for.

Embracing life as it *is*, requires that we accept hardship and disappointment. I have felt that it is not possible to truly clinch joy on the deepest level unless we also face adversity. Some would disagree with me, I know.

Children's fears are learned, or at the very least validated. Parents "write" so many things on their children. When a child is in the womb they experience the chemical reaction of their mother's emotions. When a child is present they sense the effect of their parents' reactions to life. They listen passively and learn actively. They assimilate and emulate; they long for their parents' acceptance and love. Unfortunately, this process often involves adopting racism, prejudice and bigotry. Categorization is comfortable, but not always relevant, and rarely loving.

Japan can be a lonely place. If you are already feeling alone, it can be the sad country song that sends you over the edge to tears. Even as a woman in my mid-forties, I find myself longing for home, not the one I have created but the one I was born to. I long for the simplicity of my mother's home: a warm cup of tea, a shoulder on which to rest my head, warm afternoon sun flooding through the curtained window. Remember the silence there? Remember the days of a youthful summer when you actually believed life was boring? Perhaps those were the times of simplicity, when the gap of silences existed, when the thoughts in my head were quiet.

Ironically, in this place of aloneness, I have discovered that I am not alone at all. Some time, very long ago, I made a choice to be alone in this world. As a child, I experienced myself as unimportant, and as an adult I lived out that story.

The black sky creeps along the driveway. The blue silhouetted sky melts behind the trees and I am alone. I am the last one to be picked up from the farmhouse babysitter, the place where I spend my afternoons, and early evenings. It is only 5:20 but the New England sky is completely dark, the onset of winter. I stand in the mirroring window, counting the headlights that come up the hill and pass by the long driveway. My mother is working now. She started in the fall when I began kindergarten. My father died, and my mother left to go to an office somewhere. Did I do something wrong? Did they not enjoy spending time with me? In solitude, confusion abounds. And where is my brother?

When my mother arrives, she has a special treat for me – the warmth of her hug and an occasional cookie saved from her packed lunch. I sit in the middle of the front seat of our station wagon, snuggled into the small of her arm, as she drives with one hand. Her high voice asks every detail of my day. She is truly present, happy questioning, laughing at my stories.

Yet somehow this seven year old decided she was unimportant. A single mother, who goes to work to provide for her family, teach a lesson of survival and growth, and create a home filled with joy, stability and means, somehow gets misinterpreted as not needing her children. Sounds unfair but seven year olds cannot rationalize their way out of changes that profoundly impact their lives. We create meaning about the events that happen in our youth, meaning we are quite unaware of, and then we go out and create, react to, and destroy relationships based on these childhood "lessons."

For me, the time I spent in Japan in my twenties and again now reveals for me that I am not like everyone else. My strong expectation to assimilate, be accepted, is confounded by those same desires in childhood. My stories of being unimportant and of being different from everyone else, have made me highly independent and have made me operate from a place of "not needing anyone." At the same time, I experience great rejection from not being accepted as part of a group. Essentially, I tell you that I don't need you, I'll be okay on my own, and then I am crushed when you don't need me back.

The price I have paid for these stories in my relationships is profound. It prevents me from truly getting close to those I seek connection with. I assure you that the people I love experience love and a sense of closeness in our relationship, or at least that is what they would tell you. I give and I invest time, but

127

ultimately there is always this arm's length distance between them and me. Because I experience that I must be strong and independent, I don't really allow others to contribute to me. You might call this stubbornness, but actually it's a narrative about having it all figured out on my own, and trying to prove that to everyone else by attempting to always be right. I operate from a place of believing you will leave me if you discover that I'm not perfect, and yet I am profoundly aware of my imperfections. I spend a ton of energy, resources and time trying to convince the world that I'm okay on my own and that I don't need anyone to survive. Doesn't sound very loving, does it? It sounds like it's all about me, actually. I realize that I have been spending a lot of time trying to appear loveable, worthy of friendship and connection, instead of actually loving those who are in my life.

CHAPTER TWENTY

HIGASHI CHIBA STATION, CHIBA, JAPAN
JANUARY, 2013

RIGHT LIVELIHOOD

My feet ache. The skin is cracking on my heels from the cold and wet. Layers of skin are peeling away, dry and raw. A late snow blankets the yard outside of my window. I am in the middle of my rotation of week-long begging for our livelihoods. Standing for up to eight hours each day, I am wearing thick strips of white linen material wrapped around my feet and up my legs. Straw boots with sandal-like bottoms cover my feet and wrap up my legs, tied with straw cords. The snow in south-eastern Japan is wet and slushy, a sharp contrast to the crisp leaves that shuffled under my feet as I made my way through Central Park one short month ago. My purpose here is not to gather substantial amounts of money to support our lives at the temple, but rather to be present; both to practice humility and to remind people of the need to care for others.

I spent a good amount of my time in life running, not in the metaphorical sense but actually running. I ran because I did not know what else to do. I ran because I needed to hear my breath and feel my heart beating to reassure myself I could feel anything at all. At times when my soul was numb, the only thing that could make me cry was running. My feet hitting the pavement, my muscles burning – the coolness of the shaded trees, the strike of the blinding sun, the unfolding body of water before me as I crested a hill – finally I would break into uncontrollable fits of sobbing. I was alone and I was afraid. The fear that running brought to the surface was of the desperate kind; I feared I would not find the profound love whose certain existence I sensed. The passions of this life filled my heart and fed my longing. I would have to settle for the tingling in my fingertips – my deep fear of abandonment – until I could leave this world.

I "left this world" nearly two decades later when I realized this fear of abandonment was wrapped in an illusion. My practice at Shakkei led me to know that this illusion was two-fold: first, my fear of abandonment denies the reality that all sentient beings are indisputably connected forever, and second, this fear erroneously acknowledges that a relationship exists that could ever leave me truly abandoned. When I understood that I am never alone, and that no one can leave me abandoned, I slowly became ready to give and receive deep love from others without fear and hesitation. From the first day I wrapped my arms around this knowledge, I experienced myself and others in such a different way. My will and desire to control others' lives and to control my feelings melted away. I experienced acceptance and forgiveness. Deliberate love and its expression replaced my reactive fear and longing. Abandonment was something I would never fear again. At the moment of realization, I literally felt the blood drain from my fingertips, the fingers that long, grasp, and seek to hold and control. With the blood gone, what is left is a *deference*, an acceptance, a profound presence "here and now" in this space, unseeking, whole, and utterly fulfilled.

Throughout my marriage, I thought of and feared a thousand little deaths every day. My fear caused me to experience the loss of things that either never existed or had not ceased to be. I tried to live alongside so many things that I feared could happen in my world that would have sucked the wind out of my lungs instantly. I romanticized a youth when I had so little to lose; and lived in a daily hell of fear, entrapment and desperation. My relationship with my husband grew to be characterized by these fears and I stopped experiencing love for him. I believed that in a second, one mistake could have taken everything away from me. My fear, my hell, became the very thought of living without him. The first gift I ever received was my life, then my mother, then my husband, and then my son. As time passed, I perceived so much more at stake, so much to lose, and my life came to be dictated by fear of loss. This was the great irony of my life.

Standing at the corner of this state of the art, iron clad train station, my humility is great and my mind is quiet. The shivers in my body remind me that I am alive. The unexpected burning in my toes before they go numb reminds me that I am alive. My breathe turns to crystals in the air in front of my nose. The rice straw hat covering my head covers my eyes, averted downward in deep meditation. The hours I stand here are spent in moments of meditation wrapped in time spent quietly bowing to people who place coins in my container. A burning pain shoots up my right arm, as I hold the handle of the lantern-like container in which people place money. To escape the pain I lower my eyes and focus on my breath. From time to time, I shift holding the container with my right and left hands. I must empty the container's slim contents from time to time to an inner pocket inside of my clothing. Most of the coins are 100 yen.

The sun has rounded the sky's apex and has just started its descent behind gray clouds. The station is quiet after the lunch hour. The burn returns to my numb toes as the air warms slightly. I can feel the wet of my feet as the snow melts to slush and turns to water. I shift slightly on my feet and step backwards towards the building. I must be sure not to lean backwards and compromise my practice. I am tired. For a moment, I think of the fact that I will not remain in Japan when the snow has drained to the soil beneath my feet, to push petals up in the spring sun. I recognize this thought and move on to quietude again. My mind is empty again. I place the container at my feet and extend my left, white-gloved arm. A few coins are placed, I bow in appreciation, and stand. Repetition marks my movement and my breath.

Time passes and the air begins to chill again. I begin to hear the cheerful, shrieking voices of afternoon children. School is finished for the day. High school students will be the last voices I hear today. The air before me darkens slightly with the falling sun. The voices before me are close now. A small group of students has gathered in front of me. They are trying to capture my attention.

"Hello."

"How are you?"

"You must be cold." Giggles follow these voices and I realize the boys are simply trying to make their girlfriends laugh.

For a brief moment, I think of William's sense of humor and his youthful, uninhibited behavior. I long to smile, but instead change my focus back to my breathing. Life is so full of dichotomies. Things seem complicated but are really quite simple. Silence. I long for the girls to return, but their focus has again become their friends. Below, before my feet I catch a quick glimpse of a pair of simple black shoes indicative of the high school uniform. Through the glove, I feel a coin in my palm and bow. When I go to place it in my garment's inner pocket I see that it is a 500 yen coin, a good amount of money for a high school student. Now, I smile to think of what might have been purchased with the money. Quiet grace flows from simple gestures which we must be willing to receive.

Sometime after 4:00 p.m. I lower my arm, pick up the container from behind my legs, gather up my walking stick and head down Higashi Street. As I walk an intense burning seeps into my warming feet. I know that I am limping as I return through the back gate of the temple. I attempt to untie the straw straps of my shoes but my frozen fingers do not cooperate. Sitting on the lowest wooden step of the eastern entrance to the main temple hall, I blow air from my mouth onto my hands and rub them together. After several attempts, I succeed at removing my shoes. I pick up the straw boots in my left hand and carry the money in my right. I step inside the dark wooden hallway which feels much warmer than the stairs below. I leave a trail of small, wet footsteps behind me on the hardwood, as I walk towards the *tatami* room which sits next to the temple office. Inside the room, I reach into my garments and empty the coins into the container. I tighten my clothes, pick up the money and walk next door.

"Shitsurei shimasu."

"Yes, please. Ahh, Engle-san. You must be very tired. Thank you for your hard work. Please sit."

Tea is quickly served and I feel suddenly home holding the hot cup between my hands. Blowing on the simmering liquid, my nose begins to run. I place the cup on the table in front of me and remove a tissue from my sleeve.

"Excuse me."

My colleague takes the money, dumps it into another, simpler can, and leaves the room through an inner door. He returns in half a minute.

"Thank you for the tea." I finish the hot liquid with a final gulp and place the cup back on the table in front of me. I bow and get up. I step from the room backwards. I am once again in the dark hallway. The maze of tunnels through the temple has become familiar to me. Finally in my room, I close the door behind me, remove my wet clothes and pile them near the door. My bare lower legs feel cold against the skin of my thighs as I sit to gather dry clothes. As soon as I finish to dress, I hear the resonating sound of the temple bell. Dinner will be served and I am hungry. My last meal was early this morning. As I stand, I feel my head spin. Tunnel vision places me at the door of my room. I follow the others silently into our dining room. Within minutes, I am sitting on a *zabuton*, sipping warm *miso* soup. The burn in my legs calms. The hot rice hardens slightly in the cool air. The crunch of the pickles breaks the silence. Tonight there is an extra dish – sweet soy and sesame spinach. My taste buds come to life as I bite into the delicate leaves;

134

a hint of the spring to follow. I am grateful for this meal.

We sit *zazen* in the main temple hall. The time passes surprisingly quickly. We return to our rooms. I change again and find myself immersed in hot water within minutes. I am grateful for this day. I am grateful for the reminder that a simple thing like our breath can remind us that we are alive. I am grateful for the knowledge that I have choices about how to live my life. Lying on my futon, I fall quickly to sleep. My tired head is silent and I do not remember my dreams.

CHAPTER TWENTY-ONE

SHAKKEI TEMPLE, CHIBA, JAPAN
JANUARY, 2013

RIGHT ACTION

The train doors open. I look at my watch –
7:10 – still dark. I remember the sound of the doors
closing behind me on a similar train decades previous
when I first arrived by *shinkansen* in northern Japan. On
this day however I do not feel the same emptiness in
my stomach that I felt that day. Again, I have come to
again take this place for granted in a way only one can
when she has lived somewhere for a long time. The
smells and sounds, tastes and quietude, have all become
a part of my every day.

I watch as dried, winter leaves further wither in
the wind, fade to gray and fall. The cycles of life and
death play out before my eyes in an undeniable way. I
am left to accept my life for what it is. It's not to say I
don't have feelings about the state of my marriage and
my family life. It's just to say in a way my feelings do
not matter. They do not change the details of what is;
they just inform my perception. In separating my
feelings, however minutely, from the details, I am able
to see without interpreting, acknowledge without
reacting, feel without trying in vein to change others.
While I care about the outcome, there are too many
variables to believe I can control everything and

everyone. I have some desire or intention for my future, but today I choose to place my attention on the present.

Twenty minutes later I enter a heavy wooden gate into the courtyard of the Shakkei Temple. Outside of the kitchen door I put down the vegetables I have just brought from the farmer who meets me daily at the next station. I join one of the others in the dining hall to clean. Together we sweep the *tatami* in silence and put cushions on the floor at each place. The others will join us at 7:45 for our meal of rice, pickles and *miso* soup.

Silently we move in line placing a serving of rice in our simple wooden bowls. I take precisely five pieces of pickled *daikon* and a bowl of *miso* soup. I pick up a set of chopsticks and walk to kneel at the next available place. I feel grateful to have this simple meal.

By 9:15 I am raking the snow-encrusted remnants of fall from under the larger maple trees that encircle the temple garden. This practice is a meditative one. It serves to challenge one to empty the mind in action and not simply in sitting meditation. Invariably thoughts enter one's mind. Hear, recognize, acknowledge, dispel. I know the routine well.

How I miss the feel of the crisp, red leaves under my feet on a late September afternoon. I miss the sole wooden swing in my grandfather's backyard where my cousins and I played for hours.

Suddenly, I am twenty-two years old, and alone in my apartment in the middle of rural Japan. It is difficult to breathe, as the walls cave in over this tiny straw room in which I sit. Longing for noise which I can understand, I pray for the telephone to ring, but it does not. I am utterly alone for the first time in

137

life. Many times I have felt alone, but I had no idea what that was until now. Not a single person within a hundred mile radius knows I exist or even cares. The one person who I believe does, just beyond that radius, has not called and will not call for weeks yet. I did not know what it was to have family until they were half a world away, literally. I am not even particularly close with my cousins, and yet at this moment I long to be taking turns swinging on my grandfather's swing. My cousin and I would swing together each holding only one rope at either side of the swing, as my older brother pushed from behind. He laughed and teased at how funny it would be if we fell backwards to the ground. This is the boy who my father entrusted to care for us, after he died. First my father, then my boyfriend, and now my husband.

The temple bell brings silence. I return my rake to the shed and walk to the washing hallway which leads into the meditation hall. I sit *zazen*. Clearing my head, I allow myself to embrace this feeling of abandonment. Defying Zen meditation of emptying thoughts from my head, I choose instead to indulge my feelings today. I imagine this feeling of abandonment as a wrapped infant, picking it up, cradling it close to my breasts. For a moment, I choose to love this feeling, to hold it, to breathe with it, to become one with it. In so doing, I detach from the emotion as something separate from me. In becoming abandonment, I experience for a moment that it doesn't exist. My father left us when he died. My boyfriend ended our relationship. My husband no longer wants our marriage. These things are simply "what happened." They do not hold meaning, in and of themselves. I made each of these things mean something to me, about me. I created the meaning and then lived as if it were the truth. These things were not "abandonment" in and of themselves; perhaps they didn't even have anything to do with me.

I feel myself breathe only once before I hear the bell again. We return to the dining hall to eat. *Nori* strips slide easily around bunches of rice and I am thankful for the strong powdered green tea. I am tired today.

The older section of the temple is dark, musty, and cold. The walls fortify a history past. Irony exists everywhere and Shakkei is no exception: these walls of emptiness have served as a holding vessel for much. In the late 19th century, imperial money was stockpiled and guarded here. Geisha hid out within the temple walls when certain entertainment areas in the Tokyo vicinity were cleansed at the turn of the century. Japanese immigrants returning from the U.S. after World War II rested here until extended families could be located and subsequent placement issues worked through. Most recently, foreigners have come to study Zen arts. Perhaps my intention also, in coming to Japan, was to hide, to escape. Perhaps I am fooling myself into believing I am here for healing and growth. Perhaps I am just avoiding and hiding, safe-housing so as to escape taking responsibility for my life.

Chapter Twenty-Two

Shakkei Temple, Chiba, Japan
January, 2013

Right Speech

Dear William,

Thank you for your letter, my angel. It was so good to hear from you and to receive a letter from home. I am glad you have put the stationery to good use.

I am not sure where to begin with the things between your father and me. It is not as simple as you think. Has he told you why we are where we are? In some ways he has opened fire on our family, and I cannot be with someone who has done that. You need to know, HE is the one who served divorce papers to me, the night before I came here. I waited for nearly a year, William. He made these choices, not me. Ask your father. He will tell you.

William, I miss you so much. I cannot wait to see you in a few weeks. I feel terrible about this time. I feel I have abandoned you, and yet I am so afraid. I am afraid to lose you, to come home, to find that nothing has changed. Please know I love you and that none of this has anything to do with you.

I cannot wait to see you.

I love you,
Mom

I address the envelope and tuck it into the binding of my journal to mail after I meet with Nishida-sensei. As I sit at his low table, I open the journal, placing the envelope on the side of the desk so I can jot notes down during our meeting.

"Ah, a letter from home." Nishida-sensei recognizes the English-clad envelope.

"Actually, it's a letter I have written to William."

141

"Did you want to share something from it with me?" Nishida-sensei asks.

"Oh, no. I am just going to mail it after our meeting."

"Oh." Nishida-sensei seems to drop the subject and sits silently, turned around slightly looking out of the window at his back.

After a very long interlude, Nishida-sensei begins, "There is one primal thing children need." He pauses, and then turns around to look at me. "Their parents. A boy deserves his father."

I sit feeling implicated, defensive, like a child whose wrong action has been discovered. I immediately know the words contained in the envelope addressed to William are intended for the wrong audience. I hang my head. My shoulders droop and my hands lay open upwards, defenseless in my lap.

I push the envelope across the table towards Nishida-sensei. "You don't need this?" he asks. I simply shake my head. Embarrassed, I am 14 again. My mother is standing holding the pack of cigarettes she found in my backpack. I begin to deny they are mine, explaining how one of my friends put them in the pocket and asked me to hold them for him. This time I do not try to explain anything to Nishida-sensei; we both know that my words and what motivates me to write them are really just about my ego. I want to make Alan wrong. I want William to know who his father "really is." I want William to know that he and I are the victims and the villain is still at large. I want to justify that I am making a choice, finally. I want for William to see it exactly the way that I do; I want to enroll the whole world in my story. I deserve to be right. Every word, every line, every feeling is about

142

right and wrong, good and bad, victim and villain. Every written word is motivated by fear, fear of losing William, fear of looking bad, fear of failure.

I simply stand, and excusing myself, walk back to my room.

RIGHT UNDERSTANDING

It is the middle of winter. Withered leaves frame the most brilliant of trees, the Japanese maple. The strong petite leaves reflect a deep red from under the dusting of snow. The color is surprisingly uniform across the tree. This tree is the prize possession of any Japanese garden; a skilled gardener delicately pours colder water into the roots early in the season and warmer water later in the autumn season in an attempt to extend the life of the color. I remember the crimson strokes of the maple leaves in the Japanese garden in the hilled park of Portland, Oregon. We were there in August and the leaves were already red. They extended ever so deliberately over the edges of a stone well. It seemed as though the hands of the maple were reaching for the small wooden bucket hanging over the center of the stone circle. William dropped a single pebble into the water and listened for the moment it hit the flat surface of the water. Alan taught him how to estimate the distance of the fall.

Nishida-sensei has invited me to join a commemorative pilgrimage tracing the path of Mori-roshi, the founder of Shakkei Temple. The memorial of his death is celebrated in early February. When he

144

decided to commit his life to sitting *zazen*, he left his home in central Honshu and began walking south towards Tokyo. He felt that commencing his practice in the context of a busy city would be more meaningful than isolating himself in the countryside. In the end, he continued through Tokyo and southeast into Chiba Prefecture. The journey took him more than three weeks. Our retracing of steps will begin in northern Tochigi Prefecture, continue south through the area of Nikko, enter Tokyo in the north and end in Chiba. We will walk certain routes of the journey but travel some of the distance by train. The itinerary spans six days.

There are twelve of us. Our destination is the last stop on the train line. It is sprinkling rain when we get off the train. The station is a single small building that sells tickets and not much more. The platform is only partially covered. A large drop of rain strikes my face as I walk through the train doors. We are wearing simple white clothes in layers. It is mid-morning. The train ride through Tokyo and north has taken nearly three and a half hours. The sky seems to hang heavy and I hear the hollow sound of leaves catching raindrops. We walk quietly together, following our leader. Nishida-sensei is just behind him. I am the only woman in our group.

We walk a couple of kilometers outside of town along the narrow, country roadside. Deep water gutters that frame the road threaten our every wet step. I remember cutting my hand on barbed wire years ago at a teacher conference. I lost my balance along a similar roadway in western Japan. A bright yellow street car flew by a group of us walking along a narrow road and I reached out to catch my fall. The rusted barbed wire cut deeply into my hand. The man behind me helped me to step back out of the drain. My right foot was soaked inside of the only pair of shoes I had. The man gave me a handkerchief to hold in my hand. We continued to walk back to our dormitory dwelling. Our leader calmly washed my wounds. The medicine stung hard but healed quickly.

Barbed wire does not mark our course today. I walk deliberately and keep my gaze slightly ahead. Tight rope walkers never look down. We arrive outside of the home of Mori-roshi. Nishida-sensei starts us off in a chanting prayer to honor the founder. The homeowners, who claim direct ancestry, invite us into their living room. We remove our wet things at the door and leave our walking sticks outside. The warm tea tastes like the countryside. We are offered sweet cakes and *senbei* rice crackers which Nishida-sensei tries to refuse. The cakes are a taste I remember easily, even though it has been decades since I last savored such treats. Nishida-sensei bows deeply and presents our hosts with a gift. They return his favor with kind words of thanks and present an offering of incense, early tangerines, and a wrapped parcel. The offering sanctifies our safe journey.

Within twenty minutes we have donned our wet garments and are standing outside of the homestead. We walk back towards the town. Just before entering the town center, we turn right and begin our ascent. We will sleep outside tonight, just on the other side of the first ridge above. There is no dry wood at our site. My legs are tired from the day's journey. We sit in meditation for some time before our simple meal. The kitchen has prepared *onigiri* rice balls wrapped in *nori* seaweed. We each receive two. Sweet *kombu* seaweed is at the center sprinkled with a few black sesame seeds.

146

The taste reminds me of so many times – hiking in the snowy mountains of Nagano, walking through a festival with the Kondo family near their home in western Tokyo, a quick lunch at 7-Eleven before Japanese class.

We sleep sitting up, each of our heads covered with a plastic coated cloth makeshift teepee. My walking stick is by my side and my pack offers little support to my lower back. I wake before dawn to the sounds of birds calling to the morning light. Nishida-sensei is awake, sitting in active meditation. I wonder if his strong body has sat so alert through the night. I shift my stiff legs and focus on my breath. All of the others wake in turn. Each of us is carrying a certain amount of food for the journey. Our guide asks me to unload the fermented *natto* soybeans from my bag. I quickly pass each of the group members a container of soybeans with strong spicy mustard and soy sauce. We each use our own chopsticks, clean them in the dirt below when we are finished, and store our empty containers for a later meal. Warm soup, tea and rice will be available only when a fire is possible, most likely only at our stops in mountain huts or at other temples along the way.

We walk slowly and deliberately along the mountain paths. When we stop, we sit *zazen*, however, we practice walking meditation throughout the journey.

On the third day we stop at a mountain hut in the afternoon. We are just outside of Nikko. I am excited to return to this beautiful place. Alan and I brought William here when he was young. We stayed in a Japanese inn that was famous for its outside *onsen* hot springs. The simple *tatami* rooms had no televisions and we played Scrabble, hangman and poker into the night. It was a welcome distraction from the bustle of

Tokyo. This time the distraction was in the other direction, from the silent world of our forest journey back towards civilization.

The hut is nearly empty except for a young couple who seem not to notice the dozen pilgrim clad monks. We settle our packs onto bunk beds and meet in the main hall. Sitting feels good. Nishida–sensei talks for a few minutes about Mori-roshi's visit to this area. We sit *zazen* for nearly an hour while two in our group prepare dinner. We eat our first rice in two days. Each perfect grain is a meal in itself.

Following our meal, we begin cleaning the hut. Normally, we would work before we eat but today's lunch was nonexistent. Our weary group appreciates Nishida-sensei's compassion. We will start out early the next morning and we must finish the cleaning before we sleep. To leave this place better than we found it is the goal. I sweep the distressed wooden floors. The wood feels good under my feet, as I miss the feel of our temple home. As I sweep, my bare feet feel the roughness of old nails the wood has settled around. I put my sandals back on at the door and head around to the back of the hut, looking for a tool shed or closet. The one that I find has a lock on the door. Returning inside, I find a board with keys in the kitchen. Several attempts later I locate the right key. The inside of the neatly organized closet smells like dirt and dried wood. A small mallet is hanging on the wall to the left. I cover the head with a small rag and lower it to the floor. My hand runs over the warm wood, a guide to my eyes that fail in the dark shadows of the settling night. Most of the nails sink easily into the wood; a few are more stubborn. We sweep the floor again and return the hammer to its home.

Our group gathers again; our reddened cheeks indicate a job well done. The damp rags we ran along the floor no longer snag on the exposed nails. The wood shines like the drops of steam in our warm bath following our evening prayers. I do not remember my dreams that night.

Our descent begins at the top of a stone staircase. My legs tire somehow faster on the stairs than if the steep path had been smooth. My knees have always been a source of instability for me, but I feel stronger than in younger days and I am grateful. As the path before us flattens, the ground becomes wetter. We come to a small shrine-like structure with a straw thatched roof and gray-worn wooden sides. Shinto adorned white lightning bolt pieces of paper are tied to the top; I smile to see the way religious traditions collide in this context. The Japanese seem to feel no anxiety from Shinto and Buddhist traditions co-existing side by side in so many recognizable ways. Nishida-sensei removes a still dry stick of incense he has brought with us from Shakkei Temple. The match lights easily and we waft in the familiar smell. We chant our main prayer to the Shakyamuni Boddhisatva. A certain sense of festivity fills the air. We have emerged from our temporary forest home. Civilization. The bustling context of a village is much more familiar to us, and even hundreds of miles north, we feel home again.

We walk the hundred steps to Nikko Bosatsu Temple, make an offering there and enter the *shinden* main hall. We are received and sit together with the monks who have gathered there. Our practice lasts an hour, at the end of which we each receive a folded fabric talisman from our temple hosts. I tie mine to my walking stick, but I am the only one. The others fold theirs gently inside their clothes. I long to hear the sound of the attached bell, as we continue on our journey. No one complains of the ever-present sound as we continue.

In the afternoon, we head back into the forest. The moonless night, absent of shadows, forces our eyes to adjust quickly. We slow at the top of a bald hill. Low shrubs and tall grasses blanket our stopping place. The unexpected dormitory bed of the previous night is far behind us. My head feels cloudy, as I waiver somewhere between meditation and sleep. An evening fog must be settling in from the dampness below. I feel a hand on my shoulder. Out of habit, I lean my head to the left assuming the meditation leader will use the *kyosaku* stick to strike my drooping right shoulder. But nothing comes, except a familiar softness I have not felt in years.

I open my eyes and look forward. The fog is very thick and I cannot see anyone. My eyes lift to find the source of the touch. Startled, I jump slightly and gasp.

"Alan."

He simply looks down at me and smiles. I do not get up, but rather hold his gaze. My heart flutters quickly. Tears fall and get caught in the upturned corners of my lips. I crash into him – here – I want to stand, to hold him, but I cannot. He presses his hand down on my shoulder lightly to prevent me from getting up. He shakes his head and raises a single vertical finger to his lips. He is "shushing" me. And then, "I am sorry." I mouth, "I know." His eyes smile and he nods. "But, I miss you," I continue to mouth. He nods again, continues to hold his finger to his lips asking me to remain silent. He closes his eyes. He strokes my hair with the love of a mother. "I am no longer

150

here," he says. "I know," I say with tears in my eyes. "Please forgive me," he says.

He is my attachment to our marriage, yet he is no longer here. The Alan whom I knew has essentially died and I am left to face the world without him.

I wake to my own sobbing. Nishida-sensei is kneeling in front of me.

"Engle-san." He is shaking me gently on the shoulder.

My eyes rise to him in disappointment. Where is he?

A sadness is reflected in my teacher's black eyes. He never married, but surely he has loved. His empty eyes show me that he understands everything without a single word.

"Please follow me."

I rise, leave my things behind, and follow him away from our group.

"Engle-san, you have faced something tonight. You understand now, in seeing him here, that he no longer exists for you in the same way. You might not find him again. Your memories exist in your mind, but you must accept him today. You must choose him exactly the way he is. He is here." Nishida-sensei points hard to the center of my forehead.

"They were always only here. Welcome him into your life anew, exactly the way he is today, embrace him, and your attachment to him as he was will stop haunting you. Thus, your journey can continue. Your body is not your soul's prison, it is the vehicle through which you may face yourself and this world. Choose to accept what is and your attachment to these memories will cease. It is time for you to experience profound

151

freedom. Do you get that?" He pauses for a moment and then continues, "The voice you hear is not his; it is yours and you must forgive yourself. You must accept the love you offered him to be the love you offer yourself. Your investment was real and now it is time to accept the love you created."

He leaves me sitting on a cliff. The night is suddenly clear. The sky is empty save a million stars shining a glimpse of speckled light onto my soul. I squint and the blackness fades, as my eyelashes select only the light. I breathe out hard, open my mouth wide and suck in the light. A million shooting stars collect in the sky before me. A stream of cold light hits the back of my throat and fills my lungs. Light fills my body and runs through my veins. I experience my presence anew, like a time before life left its imprint on my body. I am empty save white light. As anger, disappointment, and fear melt away, all that is left is Love.

I rejoin the group. In the morning, we continue on our path which is much simpler from this point on. A train station leads to another train station. There is a stop near Asakusa on the Yamanote line in Tokyo, but we will return home just after sundown tonight. The heavy wooden door is opened for us as we approach Shakkei Temple. Someone has been waiting for us since the late afternoon. We file into the *shinden*, removing our packs at the door. We each disappear later, like the sweat and soil of our journey, into the hot bath. Warm steam fills my lungs and fuels my soul. I am home, again, in a new place. The dripping faucet I usually experience with frustration, makes me smile tonight. It will never bother me again; I will accept it as part of my own plumbing: imperfect and yet just the way it should be.

Chapter Twenty-Four

Highashiyama, Kyoto, Japan
February, 2013

Right Understanding

I am at the Kiyomizudera Temple in Kyoto. Years before I stood on the mountainside which overlooks this ancient place. I whispered to the wind, "Amazing. You will always be my favorite." There were so many places I knew I would go, as I stood there that day. And now, after much travel, I can say this temple is truly one of my favorite places.

There is a mountainside garden that looks down on the temple and the city beyond. I walk up the hillside and stop at terraces of stone and weeds. Thousands of lost faces stare back at me. Small stone *jizo* statues line my path and I am struck by the number of lost souls in this world. Each of the statues represents the soul of an unborn child. I think of the mothers and fathers who either could not bring the child to this world, or who lost their little ones after only a short time. I wish that, like the end of the cicada season, I could quiet their cries with the simple end of summer. But does such peace require death? Can we find silence without death? Can we quiet the pain in our souls in this lifetime? Standing here at Kiyomizudera I believe we might be able to access that peaceful silence in this lifetime.

A hollow feeling emanates from the statues of death staring back at me, but somehow their presence reminds me of the continuity of life. One's spirit continues to live in this world through the memory of a person. I have always viewed death as a time when great wisdom is imparted, on the one who passes on. When my grandfather died, it seemed somehow appropriate that the patriarch of the family lead all of us into the great unknown. I find solace in the expectation of this wisdom. Standing in front of this great wooden structure, I acknowledge some wisdom in my own life. The death of my marriage has imparted on me some wisdom of what it is to live. At the very moment of knowing my marriage is over, I feel incredibly alive, even in my commitment to Alan as William's father. At the moment of death, a new way of *being* is born. To resist this death, will disallow a fullness of life; this was the despair that caused me to want to end life. I wanted to end my life because I was resisting the death that we were experiencing in our marriage. I believed it was the only way to take away the pain of that process. I was fulfilling my death-story. Only in truly allowing my marriage to Alan to end, have I been able to begin living a new existence with him.

Kiyomizudera Temple was built on the side of the Higashiyama "eastern" mountain range. The original wood of the temple still marks its structure today. The deep weathered wood glistens in the sunshine. It is a massive structure that seems to overlook all of Kyoto, a watch guard, a monument to the city and its rich traditions.

I know I may not visit this place again for a long time. At the bottom, I walk down the sloped path towards the neighborhood that sits at the base of the mountain. The tea shop that I first visited more than fifteen years ago still stands. There is one couple sitting across the room near the window that overlooks a moss garden outside. It is an unusually warm day for late winter, and the *shoji* is open, allowing a gentle breeze to enter the room. I wait quietly until I am taken to a small table overlooking the same garden.

I have come here today to meet my friend, Richard, the man I met more than fifteen years ago on the island of Sado. He reached out to me through Facebook after I posted a status update that I was in Japan. He has been living in Japan, and most recently has been working in Osaka. Since returning to Japan, I have intended to come to Kyoto to visit Higashiyama; receiving his message sealed the intent into a deal.

My robes possibly intimidate the young girl who seats me, or perhaps it is my blue eyes. She returns with a paper menu. As I begin to speak Japanese I sense a sigh of relief from her. The owners are the same family who ran the shop years ago. Her grandfather ran the tea shop when I was last here. Her own parents have just begun to operate the shop after her grandfather's death. Her grandmother still helps out, packaging sweets that are sold at the front of the store.

"Is she here today?"

"Not yet. She usually comes in just before lunchtime." It is only 10:15. My day started early as usual, waking just before dawn to sit *zazen*. After breakfast, I walked through the alleys of this revered city to return to a past I once lived.

"Your mother worked at this shop when she was just a bit older than you. I remember her well."

155

"Yes. She met my father here. They married young."

"He was a lucky man."

She smiles, from embarrassment.

"Are they well?"

"Yes. My father has two siblings – a younger brother and a younger sister. My grandmother has eight grandchildren."

"Do they all live in Kyoto?"

"Yes, but not in this neighborhood."

"Will you take over the tea shop someday?"

"I hope so. I have a younger brother but I don't think he will be interested. He wants to be an engineer. He is studying for his entrance exams to Kyoto University."

"Wow. My brother is an engineer. But there is great reward in a simpler, quieter life. Although a bustling tea shop might not be such a quiet life."

"Yes, but I want to carry on some tradition for my family. The problem is there are few men who would be interested in this kind of life."

"Perhaps, but you will know. The right one for you, will be interested in that kind of life."

A moment of silence follows. "What would you like to drink, ahh … I realize I didn't get your name. I am sorry."

"Never mind. Elise."

"Ahh, Elise-sensei. Would you care for some tea?"

"I'll have the roasted *bancha* tea, please."

"Right away."

"Thank you."

"You are very welcome."

156

The pot before me is a light sage green piece. I recognize quickly that it is a teapot crafted by the Kimoto family who live on the eastern coast of Kyushu. My hostess' grandmother was from that region of Japan. I wonder if it could be such an old piece. The random cracks throughout the finish hint that might be the case. The granddaughter pours me hot tea.

"It is a beautiful teapot. Thank you."

"It is my grandmother's."

"May I please have one more teacup? A friend will be joining me."

"Of course."

The hot tea steams in my hands. A light rain begins to fall on the moss outside. I ask to leave the window open, although the breeze is chilly. The green blanket in the garden is thick and vibrant. The roots of moss grow deeper in the silt below, years of dead moss layered beneath. The rain paints a shiny lacquer over the landscape. The teapot was a perfect choice for this day.

My hostess arrives again at my table with an elaborate tray of beautiful sweet cakes, dried fruits, and nuts.

"From my mother," she simply says.

"Please thank your mother for me. They are delectable."

"Please enjoy."

The dried persimmon is early in the season, a rare treat.

Gently I feel the warmth of a hand on my shoulder.

"Elise!" I turn to face my old friend. The salt and pepper have exchanged places on his head, but other than this, he looks exactly the same.

"Richard!" I stand to hug him. What a sight we must be — a strong cowboy in his late forties hugging a blue-eyed, bald, female Buddhist pilgrim in a tea shop! He moves the chair from across the table to sit closer on the adjacent side. In nervousness, he reaches for my hand. His strong, tan fingers wrap completely around my hand. For a long minute, we just look into each other's eyes. My eyes avert from shyness, while my smile holds strong.

My new friend approaches our table to pour tea for Richard. She brings two sweet bean cakes. The cakes have been molded into maple leaves painted with orange, red and gold leaf.

"Beautiful, huh?"

"Yes. The maple leaf is amazing."

"I didn't mean the cakes."

I blush embarrassed.

"No, really. You look amazing, Elise-chan."

"Do you like my new haircut?"

"It's perfect. As long as it shows off your eyes."

I smile and hold his eyes in mine.

"So, tell me everything, Elise."

We slice through the cakes with small bamboo spoons, as I begin to speak. Long sips of tea follow, a perfect marriage of culinary delights. Closing my eyes for a minute, a flood of memories is released by this taste.

There is quiet movement behind the counter, and I look up to recognize the kind, chiseled face of my hostess' grandmother. I smile to myself and tell

Richard of the specialness of this place. I find myself talking too much, out of nervousness, unsure of what to say and wanting to fill the silences.

The woman arranges herself at a side table with all of her necessary supplies. Her oversized hands hint at a lifetime of hard work and great dexterity. She works slowly but deliberately. Each of the packets of sweets that she assembles is perfectly arranged. Her granddaughter brings her a simple cup of steaming tea after she has been working for some time. They chat for a minute. Her grandmother looks up at me, smiles faintly and bows her head. I return the gesture. We finish almost all of the treats laid before us, leaving a few to indicate they had offered enough.

Richard and I laugh together for more than an hour. After two pots of tea, we rise together to take a walk through the quiet neighborhood. We spend the entire afternoon and evening together. At dusk he returns to my Japanese style *ryokan* hotel with me. We lay out futons, turn out the lights and talk quietly in the dark until the first lights of morning. His hand rests gently over the curve of my hip, as I lie on my side facing him. As our eyes slowly close, he places a single kiss on my cheek. I smile myself to sleep.

In the morning, we agree to meet in Nikko in a few days before I return home to the States and to William.

Our farewell at the train station just before noon is filled with both solace and anticipation. Together we look at the train schedule from Tokyo to Nikko, agreeing on a day and time. He reaches out for my hand and places a good luck charm from Kiyomizudera Temple in my palm. "I know it's your favorite." He must have visited the temple shop to buy it before coming to the tea house yesterday.

"I am so happy to see you again," I confess looking up at him.

"Amazing. I am so thankful I finally got myself up on Facebook."

"Yeah. I could have saved myself a lot of heartache if it had been around decades ago."

"Bless the broken road," he says staring into my eyes.

"When do you return to the States?"

"In three months, maybe four."

"It is amazing you have been living here."

"What are the chances? But three years is enough. I'm ready to head back. Elise, I have something I need to tell you."

Suddenly, I realize what time it is. Distracted, I blurt out, "My train leaves in 3 minutes." I realize Richard has just shared that he has something to tell me. "I'm sorry, Richard, I am just so distracted by seeing you and then leaving. It doesn't feel like I should go."

"You don't have to go," he pleads.

"Oh, yes I do. I have to get you back for deserting me on that beach in Sado twenty years ago."

"Very funny."

His face becomes serious for a moment, his black eyes intent on mine. "I can't wait for Friday."

"Me to," smiling. "Wait, what do you have to tell me?"

"No, it can wait for Friday. Go. Run." He reaches out and kisses me on the cheek, slipping a note into my hand. He is telling me to go, but his hand stays wrapped firmly around mine.

I pull away and walk as if through molasses, turning many times to look back at him smiling. I feel like a teenage girl.

Finally, I turn to race for my train, a folded piece of paper between my fingers. Looking down, I realize he has handed me a note.

I find a seat easily, place my backpack between my feet, and take a deep breath. I look out of the window to see if I will catch a final glimpse of him. The train pulls away, slowly at first, and I open the folded sheet of paper.

He has written:

LETTING GO
1.   Chose love and forgiveness as your daily practice.
2.   Look up at the night sky and realize there is only nothingness that stands between you and every other being. You are not alone.
3.   Remember you are perfect exactly as you are.
4.   Forgive yourself with every star in the night sky.
5.   When anger and disappointment go, all that is left is love.
6.   Create. The blank canvas of this night will explode into a dawn.
7.   Be vulnerable. You are safe.
8.   Breathe. The only reality you have is this moment.

As I sit looking out of the window of the train, I begin to smile. Such ease fills my heart, and I cannot stop smiling. I feel suddenly happy. All at once, life appears simple. In a moment, I realize more of what Nishida-sensei has been sharing with me for the last weeks. Letting go of the past, does not mean that any part of my experience or any part of who I am dies. Letting go, allows me to be present with what *is*, allowing me to actually live right now.

An incredible sense of peace overwhelms me. Thinking of Alan, for this moment, I feel a profound sense of love for him. I whisper, "I choose you, Alan, exactly as you are." I take out my journal and write.

I choose you, Alan

I choose my family

...exactly the way it is.

I read and reread what I have just written. It resonates. Somehow, as I read the words, I realize I can live with this. I can accept these things, and I can create my life, my family, and my happiness. For the first time in over a year, I know I can live this life exactly the way it is, and that I can create from this place of acceptance.

CHAPTER TWENTY-FIVE

CHIBA, JAPAN
FEBRUARY, 2013

RIGHT CONCENTRATION

The next three days pass slowly. I spend time saying farewells to my friends at the tea shop, the *shoji* shop, the adjacent Shinto shrine, the local fruit stand, but most of my time is spent trying to capture the present. The excitement in my belly is in anticipation for the weekend. Intention for the future with attention to the present, easier said than done.

When I return back from one of my farewell missions, an envelope is lying on the floor just inside of the *shoji* door. I place the bag containing tea I have purchased to bring to Richard on Friday in my closet and sit back on the *tatami*. The envelope contains a brief note from Nishida-sensei asking me to come to his quarters before evening meditation today. I am sure he wants time to say his own farewell. My life has become simple, structured, and seemingly safe in the last month and a half. I am very nervous about the imminent return to my reality and wonder how I will take the things I have learned about myself and my journey and apply them to my life in the States, my family life, and my practices of healing.

Nishida-sensei is in a particularly jovial mood as I enter.

"Engle-san, please come in."

He has arranged for us to sit at the low table by the window instead of our usual arrangement in front of his low desk. Hot tea is already steeping in the cast iron pot in the middle of the table.

"So, how do you feel?"

"Nervous. Excited to see William. The time I have spent here has been very important for me. Thank you for your kind hospitality."

"Engle-san, there is much for all of us to thank you for. You have left quite an impression on our humble community. Thank you."

"It has been my pleasure."

"Matsuda-san tells me that you are leaving tomorrow morning, that you have friends to visit in the north before leaving for New York on Monday."

"Yes. A friend of mine from years ago who has been living in Osaka for the past three years."

"Ah, well, Nikko is very beautiful, particularly this time of year."

"Yes."

"So, there are a few things I hope to discuss with you. You have accomplished much in your practice here. I encourage you to continue your daily practice sitting *zazen* when you return home. It is not an easy practice but it is a good one. There are many things you have learned here and surely you feel differently than when you arrived, but please understand that much time will have been wasted if you do not continue on the path you are on."

"Yes." I bow in acknowledgement of what Nishida-sensei is sharing with me.

He continues. "Also understand that you are mourning a certain death in your life. It is important

164

that you face this process with silences in your life and clarity in your mind. I am encouraging you not to enter another relationship quickly. Be with yourself and allow your mind-body to heal. This will be very difficult because the loss that you feel is very painful, but the strength and wholeness that you will experience are beyond value in your journey. You have much to give another person, but take your time."

It is very difficult for me to hear Nishida-sensei's words of advice, and yet I know he is right.

"Many great opportunities come before us and sometimes we feel the timing is wrong. Please understand that our journey in life is not like this. We do not miss opportunities. A portion of our journey that is necessary for our growth will present itself time and time again. We must be ready to receive it, or surely we will miss the opportunity. Take your time. The universe will unfold as it should and those who truly value us will wait for us to be ready."

My face must have softened but Nishida-sensei pauses and looks into my eyes for a minute.

"Remember, you are not alone. The universe surrounds you and holds you with great care. Walk slowly and deliberately, with honesty and openness. Surrender to the perfection of today."

He pauses for a moment and bows slightly. I realize our time together is finished. I rise slowly, walk a few steps to the side of the table, and return to my knees bowing deeply in reverence for his kindness and generosity.

"There is one thing more, Engle-san."

Nishida-sensei reaches underneath the table to the side of where he sits. He hands me a small, beautifully wrapped package the size of a book, only much lighter.

"Please take this for your home. To remind you of the important journey you make."

"Thank you very much, Nishida-sensei... for everything."

"You are most welcome, Engle-san."

Slowly, I back out of the room, bow one more time from outside of the *shoji* panel, and slide the door closed. Feeling quite emotional, I return down the hall very slowly, taking in the rough feel of the thick, wooden floor panels beneath my feet and the warm smell of straw *tatami* in sunshine coming from each of the west-facing rooms I pass.

Back in my room, I slowly unwrap the thick folds of handmade paper that envelope the gift. The package contains a richly framed, charcoal penciled representation of the – cicada. Just above the rust colored mat, the artist has written, "Much beauty surrounds certain death." A faint signature on the bottom right of the mat reads, "Shintoku Nishida."

CHAPTER TWENTY-SIX

SHAKKEI TEMPLE, CHIBA, JAPAN
FEBRUARY, 2013

Nishida-sensei is methodical in his practice. That is, until he wants to teach humility and then he asks the right questions to ensure his students' worlds come crashing down. Suddenly everything you have come to take for granted is no longer a given. For the past year, beginning with studies with Dai-en, my practice has focused diligently on the eight-fold path of the Buddha: **Right Thought, Right Mindfulness, Right Effort, Right Livelihood, Right Action, Right Speech, Right Understanding, and Right Concentration.**

By the time the second full moon crests the horizon behind the temple walls, it becomes clear to me that my time here was not going to produce a quick fix. My practice will entail a lifetime commitment to creating space in my life for listening, learning and experiencing that which is never silenced – my voice, the voice of something greater than me, the universe. The eight fold path is not a linear journey that begins at one and ends at number eight. One never "completes" the path exactly. The eight-fold path is often visually represented as an eight pointed nautical wheel. It should be understood as a multi-dimensional matrix. The practitioner follows each dimension of the path simultaneously, living according to each precept until death or enlightenment, with neither state as his goal. Rather the practitioner's ultimate goal is the path and not what following the path might achieve directly.

Yet, at the end of my month-and-a-half here, the focus of discussions at my intermittent meetings with Nishida-sensei has remained on my Right Thoughts. The years of my life must require much explanation. He has asked that my practice focus on purifying my mind, focusing on thoughts of renunciation, kindness, and harmlessness. He is very interested in what is my real purpose for returning to Japan. Loneliness and renunciation cannot co-exist. Acts of kindness and harmlessness are not typically tested in a simple temple setting. He questions whether I am returning to Japan to run from the life I have been living or if the return is a necessary continuation of my life's journey. So, for now we seem to remain stuck on what are my intentions in this world; have I been living for myself, for my own fulfillment and for controlling my emotions and others, or does my life journey involve deepening my understanding of how I am connected to those in my life, detaching from the emotions that breed fear in my heart, and beginning to live from a point of great Love.

I long to move forward. Nishida-sensei says that I will stop bringing my past into my present, and start living my present into my future. The organized person that I am, I have kept a journal of where I think my path here will go. I fear that moving onto another dimension of this path will cause me to forget what I have learned of myself. Right Mindfulness focuses on an awareness of one's deeds, words and thoughts. Being in a temple setting allows the practitioner to slow his world to the point where he can become aware of his actions, and of his spoken and unspoken words. Ultimately, these thoughts, words and deeds should be focused around promoting good in the world.

The physical work at the temple and outside of the temple community is the focus of Right Effort. We work at promoting life that is devoid of deadly weapons, including intoxicants or poisons, and of exploiting people or animals.

Our direct practice of Right Livelihood is in begging. This practice is both revered and shunned in proud Japan. This work is not simple and is most often done in the face of the bustling Japanese train station. The purpose of this place is to interface with the greatest number of people to remind them of others in the world who are needy. We stand quiet and faceless. Our greatest number of contributors is the elderly who, in their wisdom, understand the importance of this tradition.

I imagine that Right Action will be my hardest path. Seeking control for self-serving purposes has been the greatest challenge of my life. Operating from a place of trying to minimize fear and prevent abandonment, I have hurt others, sometimes without remorse. This does not mean I have killed or stolen, but I have lived at times with a sense of things due to me. Because I have experienced hurt by others, I have felt at times that things were owed to me – happiness, love, money, a second chance. The routine of my life at the temple has served to break down my sense of deserve.

I have never relished in other people's unhappiness or failure, but in longing to be accepted by the many circles in which I have operated, I have not always been aware of the implications of my actions with regard to Right Speech. In Buddhism, the practitioner must refrain from lying, stealing, harsh words, and gossip. My anger and sense of distrust have not always afforded me innocence in this area. At times, the necessary politics of temple life have shown me that near isolation does not prevent conflict, for we can never fully isolate ourselves no matter how great the incentive is to hide.

Ultimately, I have learned that the true goal of my life is death. Physical deaths and ends of chapters in my life have already set me off in an understanding of the reality of who I am. Right Understanding of my life compels me to accept that I am in a physical body that dies a little bit every day as I journey towards the end of my life. The cicadas of the late summer remind me that death is imminent. For some, life lasts a few short months and for others it spans a century. In either case, physical limitations, vulnerability and frailty are important metaphors for our finite lives and our every-dying bodies. There is an important lesson to learn from these creatures whose short lives remind us that beauty can be found in death. The song of the cicada denotes an impending death, as it sings for its ultimate purpose, procreating, participating in the great cycle of life and death. There is no resistance to this natural phenomenon. Nor is the cicada aware of the beauty of its song, its deliberate action, its purpose. It simply is. The result of this "being" is a participation in the most natural of all cycles, birth and life and death. In order to accept my journey in this life, I must be willing to accept the death of certain ways that I have chosen to live and the death of certain relationships within my life.

The practice of the eightfold path is the eighth dimension itself of Right Concentration or meditation. For now I sit. When I feel something, I sit. When I feel nothing, I sit. When I am lonely, happy, lost, confused – I sit. For now I sit. In sitting, I remain open and willing to accept certain deaths in my life. I accept the practice that allows me to experience life anew. For I have found that there are few practices in my life that are more natural than the ability to fully accept endings as well as beginnings with love and compassion in my everyday life.

CHAPTER TWENTY-SEVEN

SHAKKEI TEMPLE, CHIBA, JAPAN
FEBRUARY, 2013

The news came unexpectedly. The morning was a blanket of fog. Iced branches slowly revealed their glistening sleeves through the warming morning. The day seemed like nothing more than a mid-February morning; the children blowing crystals into the air as they walked to school. Vapor: dew to fog, exhalation to air, life to soul. Her essence flowed from her body like the morning fog into the heavens.

Nishida-sensei calls me into his office after morning meal. He was absent from the morning chores, I noticed. He tells me he received a phone call before dawn. Dai-en is dead.

"You should take some time today. Be quiet."

I nod in agreement. I feel silent; nothing to say. I loved her. She was my teacher. The only place I want to be is in my tatami-clad room. The only person I want to be with is me. The only thing I want to do is cry.

"What arrangements has she made?"

"Her ashes will be laid here but not until O-bon in August. We will begin an eight day fast at sundown tonight."

"She will be missed." We sit in silence for some time. I am shocked by the news of my dear friend. She was only in her mid-sixties and seemed to be in good health.   Apparently she did not suffer; a stroke in her sleep.

I raise my eyes to look at Nishida-sensei.   "I am sorry.   She was your student.   I know she had an important history with Shakkei."

"Yes, she will be missed.   And yet, somehow, in here death, she will be more present.   We have missed her all of these years.   Now she is already home."

He walks over and places his hand on my shoulder.   He feels fatherly at this moment.   There is more silence.   He lets go and walks out of the room to his chambers.   I sit.   I cannot move.

I sit for some time.   When I stand the sun is already rising in the sky and no longer streaming into the windows.   My thoughts are jostled by my ignored responsibilities.   I walk ghost-like through the corridors to return to my room.   Outside of my room, I splash my face with cold water and rinse my mouth.   The water falls in beads to the aluminum below, floats suspended on the water's surface and empties into the drain.   Each bubble pops as it is drawn under the narrow surface and siphoned through the drain hole; a metaphor for our brief lives.

Suddenly I remember the late morning train I have surely missed by now.   Richard will be waiting at the station before long.   I walk to the business office and ask to use the telephone.

"Excuse me, my name is Elise.   I am calling to leave a message for a man named Richard Elway.   I am to meet him at your hotel this early afternoon, but I am unable to come.   Please ask him to call me at the Shakkei Temple in Chiba."   I give the woman on the receiver my telephone number and set down the telephone.

173

Two hours later I am called to the office from my room.

"Richard?" I immediately break into tears as I hear his voice.

"What happened? Are you crying?"

"Richard, I'm sorry. Dai-en has died."

"Oh, Elise, I am sorry." He pauses for a moment, and then, "What do you need? Where are you?"

"I am still in Chiba. Nishida-sensei told me just this morning."

"What will you do?"

"I will begin the fast tonight. I must return to Pennsylvania Monday to assist with arrangements for her."

"Of course." A long silence follows. We are both disappointed for our change of plans. Knowing I will not see Richard before I go feels overwhelming.

"I am sorry, Richard."

"Elise, don't even think about it. We will find another time."

"Richard, will you please come to visit me in New York ... when you return?"

"Of course, Elise. Please call when you are safely home."

"I will. Richard, I ..." I am not sure how to finish the sentence.

"I know, Elise. I know."

We are silent for another moment.

"No, let me say it, please."

"Of course."

"I ... I'm disappointed."

"I know." He pauses for a moment and then says, "Please travel safely, Elise." The conversation feels like a goodbye to me. I pause, silently, to breathe into the abundance and safety of the universe.

"This is just a delay," I am surprised to hear my voice say aloud.

Richard laughs lightly in the receiver, and I hesitate for a minute.

Richard's laughter melts into words. "I will see you in New York."

"I know." I place the phone down on the receiver. A sudden realization pours over me. Richard has still not told me what he said he needed to share when we stood on the train platform in eastern Kyoto. A hollowness fills my stomach, fearing it is something bad.

CHAPTER TWENTY-EIGHT

MOUNT NISHIYAMA, SOUTHERN ALPS, JAPAN
FEBRUARY, 2013

The silence is interrupted by the sound of wet leaves under our feet. It has rained all day. It barely lets up. We are wet and we will remain wet until we return. My body has gone to chills. Moving warms me, but when we stop I am unable to control my shoulders. It is the end of the day. Our memorial pilgrimage will last until sundown tomorrow, if the sun ever reveals itself. We each hold a single rock in our dripping hands. Mine is a treasure I had taken with me from Dai-en's garden in western Pennsylvania. I have carried this rock around with me in my change purse for two years. The others each hold a single pebble from the garden of Shakkei Temple. Tomorrow morning at sunrise we will each place our stone on a pile at the top of Mount Nishiyama. The collection will mark the place where Dai-en rested for a time, on this earth, beside us, teaching.

We stop under a grove of trees before they disappear into the blanket of tall grasses, scattered with intermittent boulders. The mountaintop is covered with a light green coverlet of long blades. Each is lying on top of the next, weighed down by wet droplets that rest for a moment at the tip before sliding down the shaft. The wet mounds of grass are deceivingly airy beneath, as each of our steps finds its place on top of them. My ankles tangle easily in the long grass and I must concentrate carefully to prevent tripping as I move each leg forward.

Each of us finds a boulder on which to sit. Mine has a thankful flat top and I share it with another in the group. We unintentionally lean our backs against one another. A chill shoots up my spine as the wet cloth of my robe hits my back. As I look up rain drops fall from the short pines above and strike my cheeks. Droplets fall from my chin like tears from a child whose mother has left her at school for the first time. Dai-en is gone. The air feels cold and clean and pure. This day is her parting gift to us.

We are jostled in the darkness by movement: a lone creature seeking its burrow, the wind's whistle in the trees. During the night my lower back gives out and I find a place to lie down in the wet grass. Each blade is glued to the earth in a dark circle from the weight my body. Within a minute, blades are again reaching for the heavens. I am struck by their resilience. If only we could respond so easily to life's weight.

The gray blue morning sky blows in from the ocean below. The wind blows my hair and skin dry but my clothes are still damp. This is the first hiatus from the rain. Our feet must move quickly if we are to summit by sunrise. The pebble is wet in my hands. I place it inside the pocket of my robes. This stone must find its way to the top of the mountain.

The boulders have become smaller and more abundant, as the grass under my feet disappears. The rocks take over, making my footing less definite. My tiring body leans more on my walking stick, and I become aware that I am slowing the group. One of my colleagues catches my fall and prevents me from twisting my ankle. I smile to him with frustration. We carry on. The horizon is a deep violet. In another minute, a light pink stroke underscores its place. I can see the true summit now. We are seven white clad souls mounting the final hill in our journey.

The clouds burst, and wet, pouring rain carried on the wind splash our faces. A brilliant golden light races up the hill drawing a shadow of the mountain down the other side of the slope. Each of our faces glistens in orange-yellow brilliance. The rain passes and we are blinded by the light. We stare into the sun which sheds a remembrance of the warmth of life across our landscape. I look away, blinking, until black spots dance in my eyes.

Nishida-sensei removes a single stick of incense and a match. The mystery of their dryness will remain forever unanswered. We huddle with our backs to the east to protect the flame. The thick, gray smoke swirls into the sky in a narrow funnel. I remove the pebble from my pocket. One in our group has dropped his stone along the way. He is the youngest; I can see the disappointment in his face as we each place our stones in their final resting place. I reach down to find a small rock. I pick one up and place it strongly in his hand, folding his fingers down over the small mound. He will carry this one back to Shakkei to serve as a bridge between these two places. A smile covers his face now. Meaning lost, meaning found.

Nishida-sensei looks my way and nods an indication that I should be the first to place my stone. I move through two others and make my way to our leader. My frozen hands do not part easily with the pebble. The wind is not strong enough to topple our

small mound. We bow for minutes to remember her –
her strength, her humility, her humor, her commitment.
With her life, a stream of souls has been found,
touched, and transformed. Her soul carries us into the
wind, across hilltops, great oceans. We collide with
others. We pray to affect through a listening presence.
But now when we turn East towards Dai-en, silence
fills our ears. She is gone from us. Her eyes are closed
to us forever, but we feel her always.

THE SEASON OF THE CICADA

CHAPTER TWENTY-NINE

WESTERN TOKYO, JAPAN

She sees a dark figure through the bamboo grove. Shades of bright green lace the scene closest to her eyes, and then fade to dark green and melt into the darkness. The wind blows the highest leaves causing the tall shafts to hit each other in a chorus of song that will mark this day. She is alone. She feels bliss for the first time in her life. It is not a fleeting happiness that one feels for just a moment before it passes. This bliss stays with her and she has faith in the world. She suddenly trusts those who have loved her; she trusts herself. Bliss is one of the only concepts in Buddhism that does not have an opposing condition, like sadness and happiness, good and bad. Bliss is just bliss, and she knows it will not depart.

The air is cool; it is early February and she anticipates the spring to follow. This season will be different. For all of the years she spent trekking through the muddy hills of New England, she will experience it anew for the first time. The cool wind on her cheeks runs through her skin and into her veins, freezing this warmth forever.

When she leaves the grove today, she will be forever transformed. She will act deliberately; she will use honest words; she will fulfill purpose; she will affect and be affected; she will live. She will choose who is beside her actively rather than passively. She will welcome their presence, as if they are a guest whom she has invited. *They will be precious to her. Above all, she will honor herself.*

She will teach her son these lessons. Her goal will be to instill in him a sense of confidence that she never felt before this day. She will love – herself, him, her son. She will embrace opportunity, life and everything that they love, creating possibility in every corner of her world.

She is alone at a festival on the outskirts of Tokyo. She is by herself in the Japanese garden of a botanical sight in western Canada. She sits on a lone rock at a temple retreat north of San Francisco. She could be anywhere. The bamboo's hollow shafts carry her fears and disappointments into the air like smokestacks strewn on the horizon.

Walk through the forest, listen for my cries, find me sitting here waiting to be found. Darkness, I am not afraid. I am no longer lonely.

She stands and walks step by step backwards through the trunks of bamboo, down the corridor of memories, remembering the doors she opened and the ones that she slammed shut. Today she understands anew why she chose each door and what she found behind each set of hinges. She acknowledges her reactions were that of a child so many times in her life. Authenticity has allowed her to experience her past again, from a different view. She has replaced disappointment with forgiveness, and resentment with love. Responsibility now allows her to create and contribute, where unmet expectation once permitted her to blame and justify. She will live a life she loves, living into her future, rather than carrying her past.

Walking around the bamboo to the left she exits the grove in a different place than she entered. The scene is not the same when she looks up from different places. The sound differs in opposite corners of the grove. The small bamboo whistles; the larger stalks drum a chorus. The notes all appear to be random. Now she understands they are not.

181

CHAPTER THIRTY

NEW YORK CITY
MARCH, 2013

The pink blossoms continue to fall no matter how much I sweep. Their incessant beauty reminds me of the things I cannot have, namely clean sidewalks beneath my feet. Looking up towards the sun, I see nothing but nature's powder pink confetti falling in my eyes. My life is cluttered with beauty, and while I am inclined to complain, I smile. I look over at William. With clouds of petals swirling around our heads, I have to laugh. My head is spinning like it did when I was a child and I sat laughing with my head tossed back while my brother spun the amusement park teacup around as fast as he could. Our lives pull us in so many directions. We feel overwhelmed, torn, overjoyed, overburdened, and inept at managing our time and our chaos.

I saw Lori today. She is dying of cancer; not in the same way that she was a year ago when the doctors told her that the chemotherapy had been a success: a clean bill of health, months of gratitude, followed by months of life as usual. Just when she started to take some things in life for granted again, in the way that a happy, healthy person should be allowed to, she started to have pain again. Her bones, her left lung and her brain all have tumors. She came to us to say goodbye.

A group of soccer moms meet for coffee at Starbuck's on Thursday mornings. We have missed her for a month; we have sent a card and flowers; we didn't expect her today. She covers her bald head with a baseball cap. Her poisoned body is swollen; her eyes are a red roadmap encircled with dark crevices.

She has come to tell us that she is moving her husband and four children to upstate New York to be close to her in-laws. They have bought the house next door to his parents. We do not talk about it, but her eyes tell us that she will die there. She will know her family is settled; that her children have care givers; that her husband is not completely alone in what he must face; that she can die knowing some calm. Her eyes reflect fear but her tired body does not seem to match that emotion; it has fought only the best that it could and that fight is nearly finished.

That night I cry quietly in my bed. I curse myself for complaining about the pink petals in my life, beauty that I sometimes perceived as inconvenient, a nuisance. I regain some gratitude but beside that is fear. There is much guilt that comes now with longing for a life to grow old beside my son.

At what point do you believe your child will be alright without you? Is it when he goes away to college? Is it when he returns from his honeymoon? For me, I finally acknowledge that William is a whole, complete person who has always been alright and will continue to live as a separate individual with needs, desires and contributions to make. Acceptance allows us no other alternative than what 'happens' in life; we simply move forward to another day, and then another, and then yet another, creating new possibility and living *into* our lives.

If she knew that her children would have to live life without her, would Lori have given birth to them? The anticipation of the end seems both a blessing and a curse. Lori has time to prepare for her death yet she knows that her children's family life as they know it will end. Before the cancer consumes her body, Lori must come to terms with acknowledging the things in their lives that she has been a part of, rather than counting the things she will miss. After mating, the cicada's life will end. The human experience is only one life experience, wrought with awareness, memory and expectation. The cicada has no regret in procreating, and thus ending its life. It simply does what it *is* to do. As animals, we too would choose to create life in spite of our demise.

In an email from Richard, he reminds me that each of us has pain. I agree there is no gratitude in others' suffering. I cannot feel grateful that my life does not have the same pain as another's. The things I am grateful for have nothing to do with the laws of relativity. Gratitude is a chose in the present, and I make that choice today. Acceptance follows acknowledgement, and gratitude follows acceptance. Happiness is found within the freedom acceptance affords, and is also what allows each of us to love and contribute to each other's lives.

CHAPTER THIRTY-ONE

NEW YORK CITY
JUNE, 2013

"I'm glad you didn't make me wait any longer to see you." I tease Richard across the table of Samba Sushi, where we sit Japanese style on tatami.

"Are you kidding? I'm not letting you get away again."

"So, I have something I want to speak with you about." I hesitate for a moment. "I want you to meet William." I look across the table and see him look down. I feel deflated. "What is it?"

Richard averts his eyes and looks across the table at me. "Elise, there is something I need to tell you."

I return his gaze, feeling very present to how serious our conversation has turned. "Yes, tell me. Is it the thing you wanted to tell me in Kyoto in February?"

"Yes. Elise, there isn't an easy way to tell you. I..." Richard pauses for a moment and continues, "I have cancer."

I gasp in disbelief, as my heart begins to race. "What? No."

"Elise, it is the main reason why I decided to return to the U.S. from Japan."

"What kind of cancer? Are you in treatment?" I feel panic and despair, but also deep loss.

"Pancreatic."

"But that is highly curable, right?"

"Normally that is the case, if found very early, but I have had recurrences. Two. And the doctors have said that likely, it is terminal. I don't know. It is one of those things where most days, when I have been in remission, I feel great and become sure everything will be alright, but then I have a recurrence and realize this may become "it" for me someday."

"Richard, I am sorry. Is it in remission now?"

"No, that is why I am returning to New York. I am beginning treatment again, Monday. There is a new oral chemo drug that is in trials in the U.S. and I want to try it."

I listen across the table but can't believe what he is telling me. Slowly, I get up and walk around the low table we are sitting at. I kneel beside him and put my arms around his neck. I feel the prickles of his evening beard on my lips and cheeks. "I am sorry." Richard takes my wrists and pulls my arms down slightly but only so he can look into my eyes.

"Elise, I am sorry. I should have told you. And this is why I am not sure if I should meet William. I just don't know what will happen during these next couple of months."

At first I am quiet. I just listen. I don't want to disagree, deny, debate what can and should be. Taking a deep breath, I realize I have been holding my breath. I simply say, "I understand." I hesitate for a moment, and say "I don't know that I agree, but I understand."

This is a lot to take in. All I want to do at the moment is hold him. I want to feel his cheek on my lips again.

"Can we go?" I ask.

Richard nods and pays the bill that now sits at the edge of the table. We don't say much, but get up and Richard guides his arm under mine. We walk out together, Richard hails a taxi, and gives the driver his hotel address.

Back in his room, Richard hands me a glass of wine. I am kneeling with one leg under my body on the couch. Richard sits on the other end of the sofa facing me. I place the glass on the table in front of us, and crawl towards him. Allowing my body to fall into his, I wrap my hands behind Richard's back and hug him tightly.

"I am so happy to be here with you," he whispers as he kisses the side of my head.

"I want you to meet him." Richard pulls his head back to look into my eyes.

"Ok." He nods and holds my gaze. "Ok."

For a long time, we lay together, holding each other, quietly. I can feel his heart beat against mine, and the warmth of his breath against my head.

After a while, Richard pushes me back a bit, and without saying anything, rises from the sofa, taking my hand. We walk into his bedroom and begin kissing. Although I have not been with another man in more than a decade, this feels so right and I know that I want to be with him more than anything.

Suddenly, Richard stops kissing me and just holds me tightly. "Elise, I am not going to do this. I want this more than anything, but this is not fair to you."

I look up at him and shake my head. A smile washes over my face. "Richard, that day in Sado on the beach was a long time ago. The platform in Kyoto feels like a long time ago. I'm not missing another chance to be with you."

Richard hesitates for a minute, staring into my eyes, and smiles too.

CHAPTER THIRTY-TWO

NEW YORK CITY
JULY, 2013

It is hot, even by 8:00 a.m. William comes in from walking our new puppy, as I pour my first cup of coffee and sit on a chair at the marble island in the center of our kitchen. He walks over and gives Caper a treat from the cupboard.

After he puts Caper back into his crate for a rest and drink of water, I ask him to sit with me for a minute.

"William, there's someone I want you to meet today." For a moment the butterflies in my stomach create a sense of urgency, and a rush washes over me remembering Richard will die, perhaps, soon.

"Yeah. Ok. Who is it?"

"Remember that guy I told you about, who I knew in Japan years ago, and I saw in Kyoto in the winter?"

"Yeah." William seems distracted, uninterested, as he looks over the headlines on the front page of the New York Times.

"Well, he is here in New York. We saw each other a couple of weeks ago." I hesitate for a minute. "And last week."

He looks up at me for a minute with a smirk. "Do you like this guy? Mom? Wow."

"No, it's not like that. Well, I don't know. Well, yes, I do like him, but not like that." I pause for a minute feeling flustered and realizing I hadn't really thought about how to bring this up or how to talk about Richard.

"Listen. I like him, of course. I liked him a long time ago, but this isn't about that. Now, he is a friend. I want you to meet him because he is here and he is a good person, and he is going through a lot and I just want you to meet him."

"Ok," William says with a shrug. He seems to have dismissed the occasion.

As if the conversation was still going on, I blurt out, "tomorrow."

He shrugs again, "Ok."

I realize I am the only one still having the conversation, and it isn't easy to get his attention again.

"William, can I talk with you about one more thing?"

"Sure," he says without raising his gaze from the newspaper.

"William." I pause until he raises his eyes.

"Sorry, Mom. Yeah, what is it?"

"There is something I need to tell you about Richard." I hesitate for a moment and think about how green William's eyes are. The sun is shining into the iris and I think for a moment about how perfect he is to me.

"Richard is sick." I say the words and they just hang in the center of our kitchen between us.

"What kind of sick?" He asks.

"The kind where he will die. He has cancer."

William nods with a look of distant seriousness.

190

"That's awful," he says with a detached empathy. Of course he doesn't know him so what more can he say.

"Are you sad?"

"Yes, in a regretful kind of way. Like I should have known him all these years somehow. I regret not knowing him."

William nods.

Chapter Thirty-Three

New York City
July, 2013

The next afternoon we head out together towards the Sheep's Pasture where we have agreed to meet Richard. He is standing looking off toward the center of the field with the sun on his face. Long before we are close enough for him to hear us, he turns towards us almost instinctively, and smiles.

He has a quiet calm about him, as he offers his hand to William. They suddenly look like two men who know each other, and I am surprised by how old my son appears to me.

We spend at least an hour walking slowly together, often with Richard and William in front of me, Richard asking William question after question: What does he like about school? What is his favorite thing to photograph? Where does he want to travel?

As the afternoon sun lowers towards the horizon, we stop at a café for tea.

William turns to Richard and says, "You should come for dinner some time. I will cook."

With a look of surprise, Richard smiles and says, "That sounds like a perfect plan. You let me know when and I will be there."

"How about tomorrow?" Richard and I look at each other surprised for a minute at William's youthful sense of time and immediacy.

"Sure."

"Is there anything you can't eat?" William suddenly looks at me, embarrassed, as if he has said something he shouldn't have.

Richard reads his eyes and says, "It's okay. No, I can eat anything."

We don't talk about his illness, but instead gaze out of the window and sip our tea.

CHAPTER THIRTY-FOUR

NEW YORK CITY
DECEMBER, 2013

It is Christmas Eve, and the three of us have just finished dinner. The candle wax has half disappeared into the air of the room, vanished without notice while we ate William's duck.

Richard gets up, telling us he will be right back. I assume he has gone into the kitchen for another bottle of wine, but instead he returns with a thin, wrapped package under his arm.

Sitting back down, he places the wrapped parcel in front of him on the table.

"So, I want to tell you about something," he says to William as he sits back down.

"You've heard of bucket list?" William and I both adjust in our seats, thinking about the Richard's cancer.

Hesitantly, William responds, "yes."

"Well, there is this friend of mine. He has a 16-year old son who tried to get a summer job last year, but couldn't find anything. I guess, with the economy, a lot of the "part-time" jobs went to adults who could work throughout the year and not just on school break."

William nods, fingering the napkin ring with his left hand. He looks so cool, leaning back in his chair, one ankle crossed over his knee.

"Anyway, this friend of mine had the idea to pay his son a summer job wage to invest in himself. Together, they created a bucket list, so to speak, and spent the entire summer "working" to complete it. Cool huh?"

William and I nod, not completely understanding where Richard is going with this.

Richard continues, "The list had simple things like, he had to choose three classic novels to read. He had to plan for, shop, and prepare three meals for his family. But they also did things like built a kit bicycle and ride from San Francisco to San Diego. It took them eight days to do the ride alone, and they did it together. Also, they went duck hunting, and neither of them had ever shot a gun before."

William is smiling, seemingly excited by Richard's share.

"So, I'm putting you on the spot here, but what would be on your list?"

"Hmmm." William considers for a moment, "I don't know."

"Well, I have a Christmas gift for you." Richard smiles and pushes the package across the table to him.

"You get to figure it out."

William smiles and looks down at the wrapped parcel in front of him.

"Open it," Richard says.

William pulls the pine green paper back from a brown leather journal. He opens the cover and lets the gold edged pages flow through his fingertips, until he lands on the first page.

There are Richard's scripted letters, and they read:

Dear William,

May you live each day of your life with intentional commitment and fervor, and never forget you create every GREAT moment that make YOU the incredible person that you are.

Love,
Richard

As I look across the table in silence, I see the excitement in my son's eyes. I realize what an incredibly generous gift this is, even though in some ways it is one that William will ultimately give himself.

CHAPTER THIRTY-FIVE

NEW YORK CITY
CHRISTMAS DAY, 2013

"Why didn't you ever marry?" I ask Richard as we sit in front of the fire, sipping wine at the end of the day.

"I almost did once," he shares. He looks a bit sad, and I ask what happened.

"Oh, it's simple really. We were engaged, and she became pregnant. I was thrilled. And scared."

I wanted to ask questions, but I knew I should just listened. I looked at him and waited for him to continue.

"She didn't want to have the baby. She didn't want people to think we were getting married simply because she was pregnant. She terminated the pregnancy without my knowing." I felt my heart sink.

"She just went and did it without you?"

Richard nodded, "yes."

"I'm sorry."

"Yeah. I felt betrayed. We couldn't rebuild the trust. Or, well, we didn't. Years later I accepted the whole thing wasn't right for either of us. It's sad though. I think about all of it sometimes. Now, not having anything to "leave" after I go." Richard has tears in his eyes. "I think I could have been really good at loving that child."

I reach over and hug him. "I am sorry." I look into his eyes and our foreheads fall together. "I love you."

"I know."

CHAPTER THIRTY-SIX

NEW YORK CITY
AUTUMN, 2014

Richard and I have come to the beach for a few days. It is freezing and a crusty layer has formed on the top of the sand, as we walk along the shoreline bundled in scarves and hats and blankets.

We sit down, for a few minutes, before walking back onto the rollout wooden walkway that leads up to our rented weekend home.

"Elise, a couple of weeks ago I asked William's permission for something. He needed some time. Well, he and I had lunch a few days ago.

"You did? I didn't know." Richard smiles.

"Elise, I want to marry you. Will you marry me?" I look back into his eyes, shocked at his words.

"Elise, I want for us to be a part of each other, even after I'm gone."

Tears fill my eyes faster than I can blink. I don't say anything, at least not right away. I bury my head in the crux of his arm, and hold onto him tightly. I cry harder than I have ever cried before. I feel home, and safe, and know, although he will depart this world before long, he will never leave me.

After some time, I look up. "Yes, Richard, yes."

Chapter Thirty-Seven

New York City
March, 2015

He is dying in my arms, and I know it. Our eyes hold on each other as they did on our wedding day. I want to freeze frame this moment. I want this more than I wanted to see him in Chiba; more than I wanted him to come to New York; more than I wanted him to forgive me after our first fight. In this moment I want to freeze his blinking eyes on me more than I want my own life to continue. "Stay with me, please!" I scream inside. I will not say this to him, even after he loses consciousness. It is not fair. As much as I feel I need him, and want him, I will not ask him to fight for the life he can no longer give. It is nearly impossible for me to "help" him die, but I know I must. This will be the most difficult thing I will ever do. We have already cried together and, although he has not made me promise to stop crying, I know that I must, for his sake, when I am in front of him. When he sleeps, I hold his hand and stroke his hairline gently. When he wakes I hold his hand and help him to drink water.

"If there are people who want to say goodbye, you should tell them to come." The doctor tells me the end is near. William comes to the hospital, and goes, and comes again. He hugs me in the hallway. I break down in his arms, like I was the daughter seeking solace in my own parent's arms.

"I'm sorry. I should be strong for you."

"Mom, it is okay. He is a great man. You have been so strong through all of this."

"I love you."

"I love you, too … all the way to the moon."

He hugs me for a long time. The embrace seems to impart some strength.

"Thank you."

"I love you, Mom."

"I love you, too."

"I'll see you at home. I'm making you dinner. It will be ready by 7. Please come take a shower. We'll come together in the morning to help bring Richard home."

I have not left the hospital for two days. Richard is coming home tomorrow. All of the arrangements have been made. William met the nurse at home this afternoon to let her in to set everything up for him. I have ordered a full sized hospital bed so I can lie beside him.

For the next two days, life is simple. Mornings and afternoons are spent quietly together. I open my eyes to find him looking at me. The morning sun is streaming in through the window and across the bed. I smile at him and close my eyes again. I nestle into his side. I know Richard would say there is perfection in this moment. I think for a moment about how happiness seems to bring with it threat. The more joy you have, ironically, the more you have to lose. We do not count our successes by the increase in stakes, but ultimately that is what we have. I have always believed you must embrace the joys because even the good times will go. Thinking of all of the years we did not spend together overwhelms me, but this I cannot change. For now, I can just nestle into his side.

I open my eyes. His are closed. His hand is resting on his own stomach. I look at him for a while, because I know if I touch him I will have to face a reality I do not want to face. Reaching over to kiss him, I realize he is gone. I lay my head back down and close my eyes. I am breathing deeply and fear flows into my stomach. Tears fall from my closed eyes. The pillow is wet beneath me. I lay beside him for a long time, touching him from time to time, until I feel cold. Suddenly, I realize I am merely lying beside a body. He is no longer there.

The damp spring morning in her grandfather's hospital room floods back into her. As the breath slipped out of his mouth and nose, his grip loosened; her grandmother's fingers went from red to white to pink, and he was gone from them. She imagined him looking down on them from the ceiling, as he playfully slipped through the white tiles, smiling. His love was like a breath of fresh air, so full of life and wisdom. He touched them with his energy. He taught them to "learn" even in one's final days, studying oil painting for the first time in the last year of his life. He worked hard and fast and deliberately. He was her hero. He lived the life of a cicada.

Another departure. After the funeral, she had to return to students in Japan. Her mother stood at the glass, waving, with all her good sense of what it is to be a mother - love them and let them go - she fought back her tears. She could hear a voice inside of her head, "Do not cry. Be strong for her. She needs you to be strong." At the very moment before she turned around to walk out of sight down the tarmac, she lost it. Her tears continued through safety demonstrations, and pre-flight cups of water; they continued through take-off until the drink service began. She would not let her grandfather's life be in vein. She would live life like her grandfather had lived his.

We found each other once and then again, loved, celebrated, hurt, healed, and lived. Much like the moment between my grandparents, one day his breath slipped from us. The man, who seemed to fear nothing but losing us, danced to the ceiling and rose away. I never really knew how long a heart string could be until his death. And now each day I will face his life, an impermanence I cannot erase.

I go to William's room and kneel at the side of his bed. William's eyes open. He reaches out to me and touches my face. I turn my cheek and kiss my son's hand.

"I'm sorry." I have always sought to protect William and I know today I cannot protect him or myself from what we must face. This man who has shared his life and love with us for only a short time is gone.

William sits up and we hug. I sob, for a moment, like a child in his arms. We rise and William goes to Richard's side. If only I could deafen this world and escape this empty feeling.

I make one necessary phone call and sit at the kitchen nook table. William comes in to make coffee and sit with me. Before long, he gestures to the wall behind my shoulders, and asks, "What is the deal with that print anyway?"

His question jostles me from my thoughts. Slowly I turn around and look up at the print of the cicada Nishida-sensei presented to me a couple of years ago. Funny William had never asked me about it until this very moment. "It's a cicada. It was given to me by Nishida-sensei two winters ago in Japan."

"Hmm." William is silent for a moment and then says, "Seems like an odd gift. A bug. Why did he give it to you?"

I smile at the innocence of his question and laugh to think it must seem like an odd thing to give a woman on my journey at that time.

"I never told you about it?" William shakes his head.

"The cicada has a very specific, predictable life cycle. For many years they live dormant, and silent, almost like an extended hibernation of sorts. They consume very little and live deep within the trunk systems of trees or in the ground. As they reach their final season, the later stage of their life cycle, they emerge and become incredibly active and vocal. Do you remember that screeching, "cricket-like" noise we heard at the Zen Meditation Center in the Catskills years ago when we all went on that retreat?"

William nods.

"That was the cicadas. They come alive each year in August and, after years of dormancy, make incredible noise rubbing their back legs together to attract a mate, and then pass shortly after creating new life."

"Hmm." William is silent for a moment. "But I still don't understand why Nishida-sensei gave that print to you."

"It was in acknowledgement of my passing from a dormant existence to one of living again, in spite of fear, and of accepting the cycles of my life and of relationships. He taught me to silence my fears, accept where ever I find myself in the cycles of life, and create disruptive and beautiful "music" with those I love. That's when I entered my own season of the cicada, living and loving.

"Will you take me there?" I look at him perplexed.

"Where, sweetheart? The Zen Center?"

"No. Will you take me to Shakkei? In August?"

I smile and tears well in my eyes. "Absolutely, yes. This summer."

I realize nothing has really died this morning. Richard is no longer sitting in this nook beside us, but he is still living his season of the cicada right here with us. His passing has created the space for William to remind me that we are all in our own season of the cicada, and there is still much living to do.

Epilogue

You taught me to be close, really close, to my world. You taught me to give without fear of losing. You taught me to let the world in. As you left to another world, you taught me to live in this one. Your life was not in vain; perhaps I am the "child" whom you did really well at loving, for this short time, "our lifetime," that we had together.